TINY PLANET FILLED WITH LIARS

a Fleet Eternal story

/|\

written by Stephen M.A.

This novel contains frank depictions of invented fact.

www.smapublishing.com/newsletter

This is a work of fiction. All characters, organizations, and story elements are fictional, because reality is too implausible.

Table of Contents

Summary Exposition
on the
Alpha Vector Incursions
of
February, March,
and the
Lens Attack of April

COAT —Second Edition, Audit Anniversary Reprint— Archived

1

The Interviewer
Pleiades Tower, Penthouse Supreme

IT IS the opinion of this writer that much of the report you are about to read is untrue.

Nonetheless, I am obligated by the parameters of both my adopted profession and my contractual promise to convey the tale in all facets as it was relayed to me, with as much fidelity as I am able to muster.

There are other reasons, as well.

For starters, I paid an exorbitant amount in coterie access fees in order to secure the exhaustively extensive interviews which yielded this mountain of lies, half-truths, and false assumptions. I am duty-bound to derive revenue from that absurd and ill-conceived asset expenditure.

There's also the small matter of the impending doom of our world and all who live on it via a blanketing rain of orbital weapons fire—a subject which I believe requires much closer examination than we have collectively undertaken thus far; even if the lens through which one conducts the scrutiny is in this case derived, of unavoidable necessity, from a highly polished crock of shit.

Despite that provenance, it is my ultimate conclusion that a vein of truth does thread its way through this morass of misclaimed veracity. Since I do not know how to explain to you the precise topography of that vein in all its complexity, even after seeing it firsthand, I have no choice but to relay the direct accounts themselves, in the hopes that you may begin to understand the stark revelations buried within their sum—at least inasmuch as I believe *I* do.

(As an aside, if, in the course of your reading, you come to understand *what it all means* in a way that I have not, be aware that I would dearly love to hear your thoughts directly—particularly because you are legally compelled to convey them immediately. Relatedly, be reminded that I have registered an Intellectual Dominion Cert with the Central Office of Applied Thought [*IDC43.991.xi.3, perpetua*] and will automatically and irrevocably acquire ownership of all conclusions, discoveries, and winnowing of bullshit that resulted from your insights upon consuming the written fruits of my investment. Rest most assured that I will accept such intellectual ownership with an exquisitely honed sense of duty bent on milking it for every drop of fame, lucre, and unending personal glory that I can wring out. In this way your epiphanies will live forever, through me. And *only* through me.

In open terms: Please, for the love of Jupiter, send a net packet and help me figure out what's going on here because these fucks are all a pack of goddamn liars, but some of them have told so many lies that they accidentally circled right back around and spoke a truth, and I urgently need to know which is which. Share every rumor, every snippet of overheard chatter, every nugget of idle speculation that's ever entered your head. Think of it as a little brain vacation from COAT's grip, courtesy of this report's purchasing license—which, as you now know, embodies both privilege and obligation in equal legal measure.

Above all, remember that I, first Cert registrant in the world on this matter, now own the entire topic of "what happened in the incursion of February" in a very real and legally binding sense, and will take all the credit when we crack the case together, while you will gain nothing for your efforts.

   TINY PLANET FILLED WITH LIARS

Be grateful that I got to it first and was able to make the investment, before some Board member could order their butler to register the Cert in proxy and bury any publication related to this story forever. Isn't this a much more entertaining way to go about things, and doesn't it inspire you to register positive consumer approval of my efforts at the next available survey opportunity? I'd say so.

Glory to the Returns.

Your having read the preceding parenthetical constitutes complete consent to these terms, including the fact that your consent was not required to begin with, per the media-related inherent indenture provisions of {*SUC.7421 Beta, amended*}.

Thanks for joining the super sleuth fan club. You are most welcome for the opportunity.)

/|\

I sincerely apologize now that the business formalities are out of the way—but also, what did you expect, a free ride just because you've purchased temporary rights to a book archive? Not in *my* Unified Fiduciary Dominion, that's for damn sure, eh? It may very well be the end of the world as we know it, but the fiscal EOY still looms over us all, with its attendant solvency obligations included.

So. Now that you are contractually bound and a fully vested intellectual participant in my Cert inquiry and this accompanying report, we proceed to the matter at hand.

This story begins—as so many do in our age of unending siege—with the arrival of Fleet Eternal.

2

Bartimus Caldwell

Onyx Hoteliers LTD., Suite 7382,
Courtesy Level Omega Plus Royale

[Interviewer]

First, let me say welcome to the suite.

[Bartimus Caldwell]

Uh. Thank you.

[Interviewer]

It's courtesy level Omega Plus Royale, you know.

[Bartimus Caldwell]

Okay.

...

Uh, I mean, that's great. Very impressive.

[Int.]

Thank you. You need to purchase 2,000 units of Class A shares just to get the invitation to apply for a reservation.

[B.C.]

I see.

[Int.]

Mm-hmm.

[B.C.]

I'll ... uh ... I'll look into it, for sure, though I don't know what I'd do with a room this fancy on my own.

[Int.]

You are Bartimus Caldwell.

[B.C.]

Yes, sir.

[Int.]

Don't call me that. I've been discharged for years.

[B.C.]

I'm sorry, si—I mean, I'm sorry. I won't.

[Int.]

State your position, rank, and assignment.

[B.C.]

Yeoman Sensor Scry, Grade III, Alpha Vector Defense of the Unified Fiduciary Dominion.

[Int.]

State your duties, in the most simple and clear terms you are able to.

[B.C.]

Uh ... I coordinate the intake and regressive analysis of real-time sensor data to monitor the mid-threat-time development of incur-

   TINY PLANET FILLED WITH LIARS

sions in the Alpha Vector, when under the command of UFD Central Board Oversight.

[Int.]

...

You're a watchsmith and analyst.

[B.C.]

Uh ... correct, sir.

[Int.]

How long have you been enlisted?

[B.C.]

I ... was assigned commission four years ago.

[Int.]

You're not volunteer enlisted?

[B.C.]

...

No, sir.

[Int.]

Why are you even allowed in the Operations Center, in that case? Or have those regulations been changed?

[B.C.]

I don't—uh ... I was not given such information, sir. Just the assignment.

...

I've been told my predecessor retired out of her indenture due to debilitating stress. Uh ... several predecessors, actually. For the same reason.

[Int.]

I see.

[B.C.]

Yes.

[Int.]

Are you stressed, Bartimus?

[B.C.]

Yes, sir.

[Int.]

Bartimus.

[B.C.]

Yes, sir.

[Int.]

Stop calling me sir.

3

Bartimus Caldwell
Alpha Vector Operations Center

DURING INCURSIONS Bartimus Caldwell often feels chained to his desk.

Though incursion has initiated in the late afternoon (within a Unified Time Stamp of plus or minus 30 seconds) for the last twenty-six-and-one-half years, all personnel Grades V and below are still required to take stations no later than 0600 on the morning of.

Bartimus hates waking so early, which may be why he avoided commission for so many years. It is to his great misfortune that he's a whiz kid with sensor analysis, and inevitably discovered that Central Board Oversight had been made aware of his talents when he was abruptly recruited (then indentured) for a 20-year service stint four years ago, precisely two weeks after his 31st birthday. At the time he was gainfully (and happily) employed in the remote sexual screening industry, but that's not relevant to this portion of his story.

Bartimus Caldwell's desk, which binds him so readily, is located on the upper balcony of the Alpha Vector Operations Center, when under the command of Central Board Oversight.

This room represents the most exclusive and highly classified product catalogs of no less than three dozen military contractors. However, those who've bothered to learn as much know that in reality only *two* conglomerates perch atop the corporate meta-structure which hides its many tendrils behind each of those contractors.

In some professions, as you know, acknowledging this easily verifiable duopoly is quite literally illegal. For instance, service personnel are forbidden to acknowledge or discuss, in any capacity, any information that might insinuate that the dozens of military contractors working with Central Board Oversight are *not* in fact plucky small businesses that have been rightfully rewarded with thick and hefty revenue streams by virtue of patriotism and good old-fashioned UFD entrepreneurship.

Bartimus Caldwell adheres to this policy with unerring docility and would never even *think* of speaking ill toward the contractors. I know this because he has assured me of it several times.

When Alpha Vector Defense is *not* under the command of Central Board Oversight, Bartimus Caldwell's desk is in the auxiliary hangar, packed in alongside the other 382 service members in the unit. In that venue, each such member enjoys no less than two square meters of personal space in which to perform their duties, of which their auxiliary desk takes up no more than one-point-two-five square meters.

Bartimus Caldwell bubbles with gratitude toward the military for providing this generously outfitted working space to its service members. I know this because he has assured me of it several times.

However, this was an incursion week, which meant that Board members would be in attendance for their usual round of post-contact media conferences and photo opportunities, which meant Bartimus Caldwell and his unit were stationed in the Alpha Vector Operations Center, showcasing the finest product catalogs of the military contractors owned by said members of the Board.

From his desk in the front ring on the upper balcony of the Alpha Vector Operations Center, Bartimus enjoys an unobstructed view of the entire room. Behind him on the octagonal balcony, which encircles the

     TINY PLANET FILLED WITH LIARS

entire outer wall of the Operations Center, two more layers of desks and control consoles are laid out, fully staffed with unit members of Grades II and I.

The bidding wars to manufacture the desks used on the balcony have been quite fierce in recent years, and a new contract seems to be assigned every other month. Bartimus has grown quite used to arriving for OC duty and discovering a brand new desk in front of his seat, though thankfully, after one long stretch of genuine UX insanity, a regulatory design decree was issued that now ensures the general layout and functionality of each new desk model is largely the same as the last.

Today's desk hasn't changed since January's incursion, blessedly. When he sits at it, ahead of him, and below, is the primary operations floor, known as "The Pit."

The Pit is filled with several concentric circles of much larger and more elaborate control desks for Grades IV and up, orbiting around the fixed point of the enormous Remote Acquisition Automatic Weaponry Replay, or RAAWR. This display represents the peak of holographic mapping technology and, during an incursion, comes alight with indicators and icons tracking the weapons fire of both Fleet Eternal and the various Alpha Vector Defense Corps. It is the flagship product of Xexon Logistics, Inc., whose CEO holds a Prime vote on the Board. It was bought and installed for the perfectly appropriate amount of #18 billion.

Bartimus Caldwell assures me that this position of corporate supplier primacy is well-deserved, because Xexon Logistics, Inc. provides an invaluable service to the entire Dominion and such efforts should be rewarded. Its products are unmatched in both quality and capability.

Xexon Logistics, Inc. sells a civilian version of the RAAWR consisting of nothing but an air sampling mechanism and the holographic display itself, which they encourage to be installed in public byways for genetically targeted advertising purposes. The RAAWR is one of the few unclassified pieces of equipment in the facility. Its position as the center-piece of the entire room—where Board members are photographed on a regular basis for public distribution—is entirely irrelevant to both its function and classification level, I am assured. Likewise the enormous Xexon Logistics, Inc. logos stamped on its base, which I am assured are *not* positioned in order to rest near the bottom edge of a typical mid-framed publicity photograph.

The RAAWR can only display weapons fire, rather than the positions of actual ships—or indeed of *any* trace source less powerful and easy to detect than a weapons blast—because no contractor has figured out how to interpret whole-spectrum sensor data in real-time in order to include this useful information in such a display, at least not for a trace as vast and complex as a Fleet Eternal incursion.

The interpretation of sensor data accordingly falls to Bartimus Cald-well and others in his sub-unit, all Grade III or below, who must find meaningful patterns in the inscrutable washes of phosphorescence data fog and estimated signal values that appear on their desk displays during active contact. This wholly subjective talent verges on artistic inspiration or divine providence, and can be neither trained nor learned. It derives from an unknown inner quality enabling a Scry to project their own proprioception onto external sensor feeds, and so glean some under-standing of what, exactly, those sensors are actually detecting. This makes the scrying profession an irreplaceable component of military op-erations—almost beyond quantifiable value.

All Scries are accordingly forbidden from advancing beyond Grade III, and must content themselves with lifetime salaries of the lowest tier.

All Scries are incredibly grateful for the opportunity to be mediocrely compensated under indenture for their unique and mission-critical tal-

 TINY PLANET FILLED WITH LIARS

ents. I know this because Bartimus Caldwell has assured me of it several times.

/|\

The incursion in question began as they always had before.

That week's participating Board members had just concluded their grand parade to the center of The Pit, and now stood around the RAAWR, waiting for the first red ping to show up and announce the commencement of contact operations.

An enormous, flashing blue chronometer floated above the (otherwise blank) holographic globe of the display, counting down the seconds to the incursion window—one of several breathtaking product add-on features that had been provided to the Operations Center for the small sum of a #one-point-five billion surcharge.

Every desk in the room already contained its own chronometer display, but the RAAWR's was much bigger, you see. And holographic. The feature had been pivotal to several missions over the preceding year, and was an unquestionably prudent investment for the Operations Center. I know this because Bartimus Caldwell has assured me of it several times.

However, Bartimus was not watching his own personal chronometer *or* the RAAWR's, because his eyes were closed, fingertips splayed across the displays embedded in his desk while he awaited the first flush of sensor data that always erupted with the arrival of Fleet Eternal.

He felt the bloom of texture under his hands a heartbeat before someone intoned over the loudspeaker, "Contact."

He opened his eyes and watched as weapons indicators began dotting into existence on the RAAWR. At first it was only a few icy white icons scattered widely over the vast expanse of Alpha Vector, quickly met by a different set of golden indicators that appeared nearer to the atmospheric boundary when Alpha Corps opened fire. The engagement was joined.

Moments later, the entire visible field of view on the RAAWR became a nearly solid mass of white. For any unsuspecting and uninformed observer down in The Pit, this would have been the first indication of the truly unfathomable size of Fleet Eternal, which almost filled the entire Vector surrounding the planet when it winked into existence. But Bartimus, like the other Scries, had known the full length and breadth of the armada from the instant it arrived, like always.

Bartimus closed his eyes again, as he often did in this moment of initial contact, if only to shut down extraneous sensory pathways and let the first swell of dissonant input move through him. Some strange, indefinable echo of *alienness* coming from Fleet Eternal. Though discerning the specific shapes of individual ships in the sensor data was nearly impossible given the density of their number, from the very first time Bartimus had sat duty during an incursion, he'd perceived the *Otherness* of Fleet as an undeniable physical fact. An unavoidable textural anomaly crawling across his sensor displays. Over the years he'd seen several inexperienced Scries lose themselves in that initial crest of otherworldly cognition, none of whom completed treatment successfully enough to return to duty afterward.

The engagement proceeded as expected, at first. The smallest flower of gold indicators bloomed near the bottom of the RAAWR, but despite its diminutive size in comparison to the icons of Fleet Eternal, Bartimus knew that this minuscule gilded flash represented the simultaneous release of millions of terajoules of laser energy, and thousands of kilotons of metallicized slugs sprinting out of just under 300,000 rail guns.

Alpha Corps' salvo spread out to touch the fog of white on the RAAWR, and ticker displays around the room announced the results shortly after: .0003% casualties in Fleet Eternal, on the way to their goal of .01% to trigger the reset. Bartimus and his fellow Scries promptly confirmed these preliminary readings and input their approval codes to stamp the report.

Reset, like always, was estimated to be achieved within 90 seconds of contact.

Accordingly, the Board members were already jockeying around the console underneath the RAAWR, positioning themselves for the solely authorized Board photographer to take hundreds of photos of the members conferring diligently with one another, pointing firmly outstretched fingers up at the display while faces conveyed the gravity and grandeur of the conflict, and occasionally turning to discuss something with a Grade XX service member sitting at one of the inner-most desks —though Bartimus has assured me that Board members who pulled that particular maneuver were most *definitely not* taking the opportunity to say something lewd to a pretty-faced subordinate.

The engagement proceeded with above-average efficiency, and was suddenly projected to end within 81 seconds.

Several Board members, having yet to secure their own hero shot from the photo opportunity, were dissatisfied at this announcement. The order was immediately given to Alpha Corps to convey the urgency of their fight over the airwaves, which would be piped through the loudspeaker, so that the photographer might shift from still photos to a brief video clip capturing the moment, which would later be distributed to the media to put a little drama into their primetime reports.

For that reason, just as the ticker displays reached .009% casualties, when the engagement was already moments away from achieving reset, the Alpha Corps radios exploded in panicked cries and barked orders while the Board members strode with confident urgency beneath the RAAWR and set their faces in heroically martial expressions cheated toward the camera lens with effortless practice. A moment of friction broke out when two members struck the same "pensive fingers on chin" pose while standing next to one another, but a sharp glance from the more highly blooded executive settled the matter.

However, even as the tickers rolled over to .01% and the performance of radio bedlam became unnecessary, Bartimus had already become aware that some of those cries were *not* a charade, and as he felt a squadron of Alpha Corps vessels 800 kilometers above the atmosphere suddenly disintegrate under his fingertips, he knew something terrible had happened.

The reset siren blared out, announcing the conclusion of the engagement while the icons signifying Fleet Eternal rapidly disappeared, emptying the RAAWR's display like a glacial lake after the collapse of an ice dam.

But where normally the entire Operations Center should have exploded into good-natured cheering, now deadly silence rang out instead, because the RAAWR had shifted to showing an After Action Report.

In this incursion, like every other for decades past, the After Action Report should have displayed no more than three scuttled Alpha Corps ships. Further casualties and equipment losses were not authorized, under any circumstances. Period.

The AAR currently showed fourteen lost ships. Sixteen thousand, three hundred, fourteen crew members.

Bartimus heard one of the lower Grade Scries sitting behind him begin to sob.

Down in The Pit, a Board member kicked a console desk completely over with a shout of rage, sending a Grade XX technician scurrying backward with bruised shins, apologizing for their own injury on the way as the erupting member stomped past.

Bartimus quailed in surprise when the lockdown bell suddenly began shrilling through the air, announcing to every single person in the room that they were confined to the OC until further notice, in order to preserve information security.

No exceptions.

But when Bartimus gathered himself enough to look back into The Pit several moments later, the Board members had already vanished.

Bartimus Caldwell

*Onyx Hoteliers LTD., Suite 7382,
Courtesy Level Omega Plus Royale*

[Interviewer]

So. What happened?

[Bartimus Caldwell]

For some reason, 14 ships were destroyed that should not have been.

[Interviewer]

I see.

[Bartimus Caldwell]

Yes.

[Int.]

So. What *happened*? What did the sensors show?

[B.C.]

The ... sensor records from the moments preceding the incident were unclear. We were not able to arrive at a conclusion.

[Int.]

Unclear how?

[B.C.]

I'm sorry, sir. I mis-spoke. They were corrupted. Irretrievable. We were not able to extract any actionable intelligence from the data records, sir. It may have been my own mistake, or perhaps one of my fellow Scries, sir.

[Int.]

I see.

[B.C.]

Yes.

[Int.]

The visual records, then?

[B.C.]

I'm sorry?

[Int.]

...

Is it not standard protocol for each flagship of the Alpha Corps to maintain its own multi-variant visual recording of engagements, which are later matched with sensor interpretations and other readouts in order to form as complete a picture of the contact event as we can, in further order to facilitate better performance analysis in the future?

...

Is it not, Yeoman?

[B.C.]

I ... uh ... the visual records were corrupted too, as I understand it. Sir.

[Int.]

Across the *entire* fleet?

 TINY PLANET FILLED WITH LIARS

[B.C.]

Yes, sir.

[Int.]

...

(sighs)

...

Tell me, Bartimus, how often did members of your unit discuss the coterie, particularly as it relates to the President, and to those Board members who hold both nominating votes and Prime votes on the Board itself?

[B.C.]

I ... don't have any idea what you're talking about.

[Int.]

I trust you're aware—being a military-mandated member of the coterie yourself, after all—that no less than three contractors announced drastic and quite unexpected cuts to their revenue forecasts the very next day?

...

Glory to the Returns? Bartimus?

...

Let the record show that Bartimus is currently staring at me with an open mouth. I trust words will begin coming out of that mouth again shortly.

...

...

...

Shall I remind you that I hold a Cert on this topic, which compels your active participation in my inquiry, superseding any and all orders you may have received otherwise, with the understanding that I assume sole legal responsibility for shepherding any classi-

fied or sensitive information conveyed in said inquiry, giving you
no choice in the matter now that I have paid the requisite coterie
access fees?

...

Should your eye be twitching that much?

...

(horrified exclamation)

Don't reach for the brandy tumbler if your depth perception is
compromised, it's #80,000 nano-filigreed basin crystal!

...

Honestly. Here.

[B.C.]

Mm.

(sound of shattering)

[Int.]

For godsake.

Madame Zhou

Madame Zhou's House, Kitchen, Ruby District

[Madame Zhou]

Does it record?

[Interviewer]

Hmm? I mean, yes, yes it does, but I just want to be sure it can filter out all this extraneous ... activity. I just have to narrow the capture field enough ...

[Madame Zhou]

You don't like my kitchen?

[Interviewer]

I didn't say that. Though I would, most certainly, like to leave here without having had a kettle of soup dumped in my lap—there, the field should be tight enough now.

[M.Z.]

(laughs)

My boys would never. Every drop of lost product come out their wage—you think they don't wanna pay rent?

[Int.]

I'm ... sure they d—

[M.Z.]

HEY! You think table eight sitting around waiting for you to sculpt that fuckin' parslip? Get the fuck out of here, serve that shit. Jupiter above.

...

Don't MAKE me stand up, Petre, you take a sandal to the throat so quick.

...

EH?

...

Impertinent little shit. Thinks his pretty face mean he get away with anything.

...

Sorry. You have questions to ask? Ask questions.

[Int.]

Of course.

[M.Z.]

You're very concerned about that jacket, huh? No soup on it. You like the fancy things, I see.

[Int.]

I ... let's get started. I noticed that all the Houses on this street publicly advertise their coterie discounts, including yours.

[M.Z.]

Of course.

[Int.]

Isn't that a little risky?

[M.Z.]

Why?

[Int.]

In most neighborhoods people don't go out of their way to talk about the coterie in the open, even when they're not in an indentured profession.

[M.Z.]

(snorts)

Most neighborhoods not the Ruby District. Your first time here?

[Int.]

No.

[M.Z.]

You sure?

[Int.]

Quite, thank you.

[M.Z.]

Ah, I see. Lemme guess, "I've never felt the need before." High and Mighty, too good for my boys. Or my girls? Or my—

[Int.]

(clears throat)

If we could, thank you.

[M.Z.]

(laughs)

[Int.]

I'd like to talk about your Board visitors.

[M.Z.]

Said you have a Cert?

[Int.]

Yes.

[M.Z.]

Show me.

...

HEY, NOBU, C'MERE.

...

You have camera?

[Int.]

Just ... just for reference shots, it's only a small insta—

[M.Z.]

Give.

...

Take this, Nobu.

...

Let me see the Cert copy.

[Int.]

Of course.

[M.Z.]

Ah, very nice. Very expensive, this paper. Though that's the point, is it not.

[Int.]

Yes.

[M.Z.]

Hold it up. Make sure camera can see clearly.

...

NOBU you fucking turd, you want picture of your own sorry face? Turn that thing around, lens goes FRONT.

...

Fucking imbecile.

...

   TINY PLANET FILLED WITH LIARS

Okay, smile now, all together.

...

Good? Okay, good. Fuck OFF now, Nobu.

...

You send me a copy of that tonight, so I can show if some Board dog comes to sniff around and accuse me of breaking confidentiality.

[Int.]

Of course.

[M.Z.]

You send it *tonight*, before someone finds you dead in a gutter somewhere and Zhou is left with no proof.

[Int.]

(laughs)
Don't be absurd.

[M.Z.]

Oh?

[Int.]

You can't be serious. Idea regulation is one of the only areas of this government that actually functions, nobody would violate the rights and responsibilities of this Cert.

[M.Z.]

Oh?

[Int.]

(laughs)
When's the last time you heard of a Cert holder ending up mysteriously dead?

[M.Z.]

Last month. And *theirs* was just a supply dispute for some parlors, small game.

[Int.]

...

Ah. You read that report, I see. It was ruled an accident. Quite plausibly, in my opinion.

[M.Z.]

Oh?

[Int.]

...

I wouldn't have thought you'd be subscribed to that newspaper to begin with.

[M.Z.]

Are you saying I can't read?

[Int.]

What? Of course not. Didn't you publish your own book a few years ago?

[M.Z.]

Mmm. No autographs. But I'll—PETRE. GO GET A BOOK FROM THE BOX IN MY OFFICE FOR FANCY JACKET HERE.

[Int.]

That's really not—

[M.Z.]

Your question?

   TINY PLANET FILLED WITH LIARS

[Int.]

...

(sighs)

...

I understand that Crowley Vanderbilt has been a frequent guest of yours in the past.

[M.Z.]

(snorts) Trash.

...

Don't worry, I don't need the Cert for that. I say to his trash face, all the time.

(laughs)

[Int.]

He must really enjoy your hospitality, to put up with that kind of abuse.

[M.Z.]

(chuckling) The abuse is the point, some days.

[Int.]

Ah ... I see.

...

Is it the same situation for most Board visitors?

[M.Z.]

Some. Not all. We have several who just want cuddle. Some like to be bound and stroked. Others—

[Int.]

None here for simple intercourse?

[M.Z.]

(laughs)

Intercourse? Jupiter above. WE GOT A DOCTOR HERE, BOYS.

(out-of-capture laughter)

Intercourse.

...

But no, 'course not, no "intercourse." You think I run a House of morons?

[Int.]

What do you mean?

[M.Z.]

Nobody paying rent to *me* would be STUPID enough to roll around like that with a Board member. Those dogs get to walk into finest hospitals, get any treatment they want on demand. They can buy whole new bodies practically. Most of them don't even bother get tested but once a year, if you're lucky. They're all crawling with disease. Animals. I disinfect suite extra hard when they leave, every time.

...

Dangle in the dingle sex is for the poor. Anybody here wants to pay a little rent by sticking or getting stuck saves it for the respectable working class. Plebs or military folk when they're planet-side or out on off-duty rotations—people who have to *care* for their bodies, not some walking pile of gilded bacteria.

[Int.]

I see.

...

   Tiny Planet Filled With Liars

And what does Vanderbilt get up to, when he's here? Does he have any favorites?

[M.Z.]

Sometimes. Usually not. My House is buffet to him. He samples, and nibbles, he doesn't take whole dish and keep forever.

...

You want truth, sometimes I think he just needs the company.

[Int.]

Companionship?

[M.Z.]

Sure. You ever been inside a Board palace?

[Int.]

Yes.

[M.Z.]

Then you know. Buncha butlers and maids and attendants and in-dentured—few friends.

...

No friends, in Crowley's case, I think. Probably because he's such a fucking prick.

[Int.]

You'd think he could buy a few friends.

[M.Z.]

(laughs)

Sure, yes. But a man like him, don't want friends except his own class, and none of them need the cash.

(laughs)

[Int.]

Tragic.

[M.Z.]

Mmm. I like you.

[Int.]

I ... thank you.

[M.Z.]

You got a good face, though not the usual we see around here. Obviously.

...

You wanna rent a room, earn a little more fancy? I wonder what's between those legs today, though. Let me see, I'll appraise value.

[Int.]

No, thank you.

[M.Z.]

(laughs)

[Int.]

So, when was the last time Vanderbilt was here?

[M.Z.]

Oh ... been a few months. Unusual, actually, now I think of it. He must be busy with something. Finding a new way to suck up money he don't need from people who rely on it.

[Int.]

I see.

...

And what does he usually get up to while he's here? What specifically? What was the last ... activity he ordered?

[M.Z.]

You saw signs on my House when you arrived?

[Int.]

I ... yes, I did.

[M.Z.]

Then you saw *second* biggest one, says, "A Public House for Private Pleasures."

[Int.]

Yes.

[M.Z.]

Emphasis on the "private," fancy jacket.

[Int.]

But—

[M.Z.]

Yes, yes. You'll need more than fancy Cert to get forensic analysis out of me, though. What, you think I never want to make money again? Take me to court if you like, see how much enforcing your Cert rights gets you then.

[Int.]

I'm sorry. I thought—

[M.Z.]

I like you. I talk whenever you want. But if you want to know about *that*, you come back here some day with a bag of bills big enough to set Zhou up for life. Maybe then you'll learn what Crowley likes to do when his clothes come off.

[Int.]

I see.

...

Well, in that case, any last advice to prepare for my meeting with him in a few days?

[M.Z.]

Sure—oh, Petre, about fucking time. What, you fall into a pussy
on the way?
(laughs)
Here. One of my personal copies, comes with a permanent book
license, it won't expire.

[Int.]

Thank you.

[M.Z.]

Sure.

...

Be careful with Crowley. You're just his type.

[Int.]

I'm not sure I understand what you mean.

[M.Z.]

You know *exactly* what I mean.

Crowley Vanderbilt

Palace Equinox, Floor 107, Tertiary Drawing Room

[Interviewer]

Mr. Vanderbilt, thank you for agreeing to this interv—

[Butler]

May I?

[Interviewer]

No, thank you, I—

[Crowley Vanderbilt]

GET THE FUCK OUT. Hasn't even touched the drink yet, of fucking course it doesn't need a refill. You blind pile of shit.

...

Tell Beatrice I don't want to see your FAT FUCKING HEAD UP-STAIRS AGAIN, you live in the cellars now.

[Interviewer]

It's really fine, I didn't mind the interruption.

[Crowley Vanderbilt]

I do. Fucking impossible to get new indents trained.

[Int.]

She's a new member of palace staff?

[C.V.]

Sure. She'd have to be, wouldn't she? I only sliced the last man's face a few days ago. Doubt he's even out of the recovery ward yet, what with the garbage machinery they use for you lot in the clinics.

[Int.]

...

I see.

[C.V.]

Why *haven't* you touched the drink yet, hmm? Some hosts would find that unconscionably rude, even when their guest is only present because they borrowed a lifetime on mortgage to pay for some silly Cert.

[Int.]

...

(clears throat)

Mr. Crowley Vanderbilt, CEO of Vanderbilt Ascendant, Incorporated. As I understand it, your firm primarily provides signals support and design to Alpha—

[C.V.]

You've got nice legs. Strong, like I like. I'd always heard your kind was weak below the waist—even if you do have more than one toy to play with. Let's find out how wrong that was.

(laughs)

[Int.]

... provides signals support and design to Alpha Vector Defense, and occasionally Vectors Beta and Gamma, as well.

[C.V.]

(sighs)

   TINY PLANET FILLED WITH LIARS

Sure. Who cares. The point isn't the product. The point is the Board.

[Int.]

Oh? I thought … yes, my notes say your grandmother actually invented the multi-phase antennas that preceded your flagship product lines, and your father was personally involved in the development of the currently deployed signal buffer circuitry that comprises your largest contract with Alpha Vector Defense?

[C.V.]

And? Oma also refused to "take advantage" of the palace-grade hospitals and died at 96 like a drooling old fool, and Dad got himself killed in some quarry somewhere. Believe me, following in their footsteps is not on my agenda.

[Int.]

I see. I thought they'd both been awarded Meritorious Commendations of the first order for their contributions to the war effort.

[C.V.]

Yeah, okay. You can buy those by the pack these days. You're welcome to peruse mine hanging in the concourse on your way out the door. Unless, of course, you stay the night instead.

[Int.]

Let's stay—

[C.V.]

I wasn't aware your Cert covered both the incursion of February and my family tree.

[Int.]

I apologize. I don't intend to be intrusive, I'm just trying to confirm the context of your background.

[C.V.]

Contextualize *this*.

[Int.]

I'd rather not.

[C.V.]

(laughs)

Fucking liar. Twenty-five centimeters, of course you'd rather.

[Int.]

I'd say twenty, if we're rounding up.

[C.V.]

(laughs)

[Int.]

Mr. Vanderbilt, I've come to understand that you were in attendance as one of the Overseeing Board members during the incursion several weeks ago, and that your reaction to the way it all played out was ... vigorous. In fact, I believe you kicked over an entire console, nearly crushing a technician in the process.

[C.V.]

(chuckles)

Oh, right. Guess she should've moved a little quicker.

[Int.]

They. I'm curious what factors may have been driving your reaction. From the descriptions I've received, it almost seemed like you had some kind of personally vested interest in the outcome of that engagement, and I'm having difficulty determining how such an interest would have coincided with the products you're actually providing under contract. I was also curious to see that your company was one of three contractors that sharply cut their revenue

 TINY PLANET FILLED WITH LIARS

forecasts the following morning. I can't see how these factors re-
late in the particulars.

[C.V.]

You've done a lot of talking, huh?

[Int.]

I became aware of an anomalous outcome to that incursion and
secured my Cert ten days following the event. I have been conducting interviews and research since the day that Cert was
granted, yes.

[C.V.]

Interesting how you might have *become aware* of the outcome,
given the security clearance applied to the entire event within ten
minutes of its conclusion. In fact, without that little Cert of
yours, you'd be looking at incarceration for even talking about this
with me, as would anybody else you've "interviewed." How fortunate for you.

[Int.]

Mmm.

...

You know how these things get around, Mr. Vanderbilt. I've built
up a modest network of contacts over the years, and sometimes,
during a crisis, information drifts into capillaries it might not under normal conditions.

[C.V.]

I'm sure. But if you use the word "crisis" again you'll wake up in a
cell.

[Int.]

Do sixteen thousand families not count as a crisis? Are they under
classification strictures as well, or haven't they been told yet?

...

Mr. Vanderbilt?

[C.V.]

Why don't you come put your lips on this and see what insights we can draw out.

[Int.]

Mr. Vanderbilt, please close your skirts.

7

The Interviewer, Madame Zhou
Ruby District and Etc.

WHEN I exited Madame Zhou's House after the initial interview—
several days before Mr. Vanderbilt would show me his penis during our
first meeting—I considered leaving the copy of the Cert photograph
with her door attendant. After all, like I'd tried to say, it was an instant-
process camera, and the photograph was ready before we'd even concluded our discussion.

However, it seemed obvious in immediate retrospect that Zhou must
have known the camera's capabilities, and upon considering several
other comments she'd made during our interview, I had begun to suspect that she was actually issuing an invitation to return later that
evening under more discrete conditions. This seemed to be confirmed
when her door attendant offhandedly mentioned that, in the future, I
might choose to exit through a side door if I preferred.

So I opted to proceed as if that instinct were correct, and chose instead to keep the photograph on my person, while taking the opportunity to have a little wander around the Ruby District until nightfall
proper.

While I know many residents of the District like to assume that the
entire world is familiar with the ins and outs of the neighborhood, I am
equally aware that most of you will have never set foot within its
bounds. Accordingly, let me take this opportunity to demystify the real-

ity of its impression for you. Though the media directors love to focus their cameras on the central square and eponymous gemstone fountain marking the District's founding, I assure you that the rest of the neighborhood is quite mundane in layout and design—though somewhat less seedy than the more conservative among you might like to believe. In actuality, the most definitive quality, to me, is how indistinguishable many of its streets are from any typical office or retail district; barring lanes where several entertainment establishments cluster together, as is the case with Zhou's location.

But the single detail I find most striking is not even within the District itself, but rather my surprise at seeing how many Board palaces are located *near* to it these days. While such palaces are fairly evenly distributed around the rest of the planet, no less than five towers were visible from Ruby's streets, including that of Mr. Vanderbilt, which is located barely four avenues away from the outermost boundary.

One might remark upon the apparent inexplicability of such property investment decisions, given the region's relatively great distance from any meaningful center of finance, government, or military manufacture. One might also remark upon the potential conveniences of being located next to one of the coterie's central-most hubs, since Madame Zhou is in the distinct minority as a wholly independent proprietor of her own establishment, while many of her competitors are rumored to be funded entirely by coterie interests.

For these and other reasons, upon exiting Madame Zhou's House, I was not especially surprised to come across a young Board member staggering down the street spraying vomit even as she walked, while the boy and girl on either of her arms did their best to dodge the back-splash (with something less than total success, more's the pity).

    Tiny Planet Filled With Liars

I was, however, surprised to see several other such scions before I'd even turned the corner, and no less than *five* identifiable Prime voting members over the course of the next half hour of my wanderings.

I found this surprising because it was still the late afternoon of a week day, and I remember a period, not that long ago, when Prime voting members were intensely consumed by the necessities of managing both government and military *on top* of their corporations, and may not have had time for such extracurriculars in the middle of a working week.

One might remark upon this change and wonder what it means for the security of our world, and how so many of the Dominion's finest contractors might continue to safeguard their contracts in a manner robust enough to withstand this sort of creepingly pervasive neglect.

Of course, one might make such a remark only if one were not cognizant of the political and legal ramifications of the very idea—and I am most certainly cognizant of such.

/|\

By the time I'd eventually come around to concluding a (genuinely surprising) dinner of braised butterwort at a charming hashery several blocks off the fountain square, night was more than an hour fallen and the Ruby District was coming to its full. Understanding what this meant for a business like Madame Zhou's, I hurried back to her establishment and slipped—with rather graceful stealth, I should think—down a small and shadowed alleyway that I hoped would lead to the aforementioned side door.

Fortunately it did, and to my surprise my knocking was answered within moments by Madame Zhou herself.

"What the fuck you doing here, fancy jacket? You get lost on the way home?"

"I, uh ..."

"Well come in, if you're here. May as well have a cup of fucking tea, or people say Zhou is less friendly these days."

"Of course."

"Jupiter above," she said while closing the door.

The bright lights of the main foyer spilled into the smaller hall the door led to, but the corridor itself was quite dim, I noticed. I heard the sounds of a small, very drunken group of friends being ushered in by the front door attendant.

One of them called out, "I wanna take a dick until I don't remember my name!"

"Oh, and fritters," another said.

"Hey door, who gives the best handie here, eh?" interjected yet another.

"Shit yes. With honey."

"Until I don't remember your name!"

This was met with hoots of laughter drifting out of earshot.

Madame Zhou took my hand, interrupting my eavesdropping. "Come, kitchen too busy to sit now, we'll have in my office."

I followed her down the corridor then trailed behind as she plodded up an alarmingly narrow staircase at its end. The walls pulsed with the bass coming from the House band in the restaurant and lounge, and now and then the (rather flimsy-looking, and quite sparse) lighting fixtures hanging near head-height shook under the frequencies. Several times, a particularly vigorous beat knocked a few paint chips loose as we passed.

But as it turned out, such interior design was a very deliberate choice, because once we reached the office I saw that it was built to much higher standards. The walls and floors were quite dingy, but of that particular type of weathering that can only arise from materials that were luxuriantly costly and durable to begin with. Indeed, Zhou's desk itself would

   TINY PLANET FILLED WITH LIARS

have fit into any Board member's own office, thickly lacquered and heavily constructed as it was, including a conspicuous display of elaborately detailed swallowtail joinery. (I estimated an initial value of at least #sixty-point-five million for that piece alone.) Its surface was piled with teetering towers of paperwork, but on the wall behind it was a solid row of cabinetry stacked in neat uniformity. Most of these pieces were the usual file cabinets, but a few were cleverly designed databanks, fronted to blend in with their more analog neighbors. Each such cabinet featured a large, forbidding lock, though I hadn't noticed Zhou carrying any keys yet.

I couldn't help thinking this was quite the assemblage of furniture for a simple Madame, though Zhou *had* been in business for a very long time.

She shut the door behind us, and it was around this point that I realized no tea set was in evidence.

She fiddled with some unseen bauble on the wall near the door and the entire room shimmered—a blink-and-you-miss-it pulse rippling through every surface like water chasing a pebble drop.

"What was that?" I asked.

"Mind your fucking business, is what that," she replied.

Then I realized I could no longer hear the music downstairs.

She brushed past me and moved to take the seat behind the desk, holding out an arm to usher me to one of the cushioned visitor chairs set in front. She settled in with a happy sigh and crossed her arms, the very picture of relaxation—holding court in her den, something it was obvious she quite enjoyed doing.

"So," she said, "you showed up. Maybe you're not stupid as you sound. Though perhaps very close."

"Excuse me?"

She laughed. "Where'd you teach yourself that accent, commercials?" Seeing the expression on my face, she laughed again. "Oh, I see, you think it's a secret. Never mind then, fancy jacket, you sound perfectly normal."

I could feel my pulse quickening.

"Anyway, most idiots not even notice. Don't worry."

"Mmm," was all I could bring myself to reply, triggering another round of mirth at my expense.

Zhou's laugh was remarkable, it must be said. Sometimes a series of low, rolling barks; other times a high, rasping cackle that sounded like it came from a throat decades older than her own. But whatever form it took, it was always aggressively carefree. Many people use laughter as deflection or smokescreen, especially in the face of questioning, but every time Madame Zhou let loose, it was undeniable that she truly meant it. I was beginning to understand why she might inspire such loyalty from her renters, customers, and whatever other charges orbited the vicinity, even despite her abrasive manner.

I cleared my throat. "So, I take it no tea will be served."

That laugh. "You want? I send for some, Nobu come quick."

"No, thank you. Perhaps we should just get to the business at hand."

I pulled the Cert photograph from a pocket and held it out. She took it and gave it only a perfunctory glance, backed by a grunt of approval, before throwing it in an open drawer.

"Now to real business," she said, leaning forward slightly in her chair. "I like you, fancy jacket. I like what you're doing. But you're idiot. Very, very dumb."

My mouth dropped open. "What do you mean?"

"Look at the way you dress, for one, Jupiter fuck. How dumb? But this just for starters. You think your Cert some kind of shield?"

 TINY PLANET FILLED WITH LIARS

"I—yes. Yes, I think that's precisely what it is. One of the strongest—and only—legal shields that really exists in this world anymore, when money comes to bear."

"Pfft." She waved a hand dismissively. "How do you live this long with ideas like that? I don't know."

I pursed my lips.

"Look here, fancy jacket, some indent gets an order to cut your heart out from behind, they're not checking your pockets for Cert first. Idiot. I invest in you, so you listen to Zhou now."

"Invest?" But when she held up a finger, I dropped the question and simply nodded, being more interested in learning what was prompting this display—even though I considered her perspective rather overly cynical, to say the least.

She continued, "You forget about safety net of rules you think you live inside. Why somebody like *you* would still believe in that net, Jupiter knows. Forget it now. Because people who believe that kind of thing, they look at Board members and believe they have all profit they need. Wrong ... mostly. Some Board members not happy with their profit. Don't *need* more, but *want* more. Always. Makes them even more dangerous. And that type of Board member not looking for how to make the *rules* work for them."

I couldn't bring myself to agree to the blanket nature of that statement, though I recognized its truth on an occasional and individual level. But I said, "Aren't you afraid to be talking about this with me? You know I'm going to include it all in my Cert report, don't you?"

She laughed. "You're not even recording."

"No ... but I have a *very* good primary memory, and I always take notes of important conversations I've had at the end of the day."

She nodded happily, as if the matter were settled. "Just fine, then. Don't matter how good your memory is, I say you lie if I need to, then people believe you lie. Easy. No problem for Zhou ... Shit, I say you lie even if you *are* recording, same thing. No problem for Zhou." She cackled.

"I see."

She leaned forward, resting her elbows on the desktop. "Remember whatever you want, fancy jacket, fuck do I care?" She stabbed at the desk with a forefinger as she said, "What people do here naked is their own concern. I guarantee discretion, as part of business. They know this. They trust this. In kitchen I tell you nothing about Crowley that anybody with eyes can't see just watching him carry on in my public restaurant. Once he flash enough cash to convince some poor disgusted fool to go up to a room with him and earn a little rent, *then* I shut up.

"But *this*," she indicated the space between us with her finger, "is politics. None of *this* is that kind of secret. I fear nothing." She sat back again. "Anyway, Crowley has plenty of his own enemies on the Board, just like everyone else. He wants to get uppity with me, I catch wind of it, then I buy some of their protection and he discover it's not profitable enough to bother with. Even fool like him can see."

"I see," I said.

She grinned. "No you don't. But I see that you listen, and good enough for now."

I shrugged but nodded.

"You do good start here, fancy jacket. But you need to forget about 'truth.'" She sneered the word distinctly. "You worry less about truth, idiot, worry more about *fact*."

"I'm not sure I follow."

She sighed. "Truth might happen to be fact, and sometimes fact taken as truth, but they're not same thing. Not even close, idiot. Truth is *belief*. Fact is *reality*. Truth is *social*. Fact is *physical*. You spend all your time trying to get people to tell you their truth, even when they tell you

   Tiny Planet Filled With Liars

it, it's still not fact. You chase the wrong shuttle. Truth does not save us. *Fact* save us. *Fact* of Fleet Eternal. *Fact* of Board. *Fact* of military. *Fact* of this world." She leaned forward again and thrust a finger at me. "You search for *fact*, fancy jacket, or you sell that Cert to somebody who will."

I swallowed heavily into the silence that lingered after her words.

"... You really think I'm doing that poorly so far? I've sent quite a number of preliminary questionnaires, but I've only conducted two formal interviews. Three, by the time I meet Crowley later this week."

She laughed. "Yeah okay, some lying Board and a bunch of useless people got nothing but *truth* for you. Just wasting time." She raised a hand at my expression and continued, "Not so very poorly in *all* ways—but in other ways, very yes. For starter, you only get a Cert for February incursion, idiot. You too poor for more? Maybe should sell some jackets. You think you'll be finished by March incursion next week? You think anybody bother talking to you about February then? They'll get whole new round of classifications after next battle, your little paper won't be shit." More cackles, now. "So, I buy you Certs to cover next two incursions, too."

I blinked.

"Actually, *you* bought them."

"What? No I didn't," I said.

"Sure, FACT is that I sent Petre to buy them three days ago," she cackled. "But TRUTH is that records say you buy them yourself."

"We didn't even know one another three days ago," I replied.

"Oh?"

I felt myself blinking again. Too much.

Then I found myself re-examining the fact that Madame Zhou herself had potentially been lurking by the side door all evening awaiting my arrival, even as her restaurant filled with night-time revelers, drunk and eager to lose money.

Madame Zhou, who had apparently just spent what was surely in excess of #two-point-five billion in my name.

Then I found myself breathing rather more heavily than usual while Zhou slapped a button on the desk and ordered Nobu to, "Bring some tea for 'good memory' idiot can't even remember oxygen long enough to matter."

She looked at me and shook her head, then grinned and slapped the button again. "And tell Petre 'fuck you,' just because."

Cackle.

The Interviewer
Palace Equinox, Street Level and Etc.

AT THE time (eight days before the March incursion), I exited Palace Equinox following the conclusion of my interview with Crowley Vanderbilt and stomped into the street, having vowed to myself that I would print each and every word that had slimed its way out of his mouth during the remainder of our discussion, once I had convinced him to (mostly) conceal his penis beneath his skirts again. However, the truth is that you've already become aware of the primary thrust of his responses to my questioning, so I believe brevity demands that I mark it as read and move on.

And if there's one thing you've undoubtedly come to understand about me by this point in our tale, it is that I—barring extenuating circumstances or the need to otherwise precisely outline the parameters of an engagement or even simply remark upon a notable component of a subject's demeanor—am nothing, if not brief.

In truth, I was eager to leave Vanderbilt's drawing room for more reasons than those supplied by his odious personage, since I'd deliberately scheduled our interview to put me in a position to take the shuttle home during an orbital window that would—I hoped—encompass the scouting engagement of end February.

Of course, barely more than fifteen years ago, this plan would have been fruitless since all exo-atmospheric civilian travel was suspended during scouting alerts, which were then, for several reasons, still treated with the same seriousness as a full incursion. Thankfully for my contemporary objective, the transport cartel had since managed to quell its infighting long enough to successfully lobby for the redaction of those attendant regulations, on the premise that a great deal of revenue was unnecessarily left stranded by their inability to facilitate tourism of the engagements. But as you know, the sightseeing boom that ensued lasted barely one full year before everybody who wanted to (and was capable of paying the extortionate ticket fees) had already seen the show, and these days it's simply the usual shuttles tracing their usual routes while the scouts of Fleet Eternal linger high above.

Given my motivations, I was obliged to put my resentful turmoil to the side, and equally obliged to stride past the shuttle station located down the block from Vanderbilt's palace, since it only berthed the most modern and high-speed vessels. Instead, I rushed down the streets toward a rather more ramshackle station positioned just outside the borders of the Ruby District, where I knew I could still catch one of the old ballistic-trajectory-type vessels, affording me nearly a full hour above the atmosphere before arriving home. Most unfortunately, this necessitated the use of a budget line, though I did avail myself of the luxury package upgrade; #9,800, inclusive.

The boarding ramp wafted itself in the aromas of digestive juices and stale liquor, but fortunately at this hour of the evening the source-points of such perfumes were still merrily engaged in Ruby, and would not gather themselves to stagger toward the ticket booth for some time yet. This left my chosen shuttle nearly empty, and I found that the observation deck was completely unoccupied upon my arrival. Though I was entitled to a luxury upgrade seat, it turned out that such a throne consisted of nothing but a single row on the deck with the usual furnishing, but every other seat had been ripped out to afford luxury passengers

   TINY PLANET FILLED WITH LIARS

marginally more leg space. Despite my duly paid fee, I opted instead for the very front row, where the seats were regularly regular, but would provide a much better panorama of the system once aloft.

The vessel shuddered off the landing pad and began its slow climb through the air several minutes after I settled in, shortly followed by an attendant who appeared to be caught in the throes of a truly existential spell of boredom. She trudged toward my seat at the front of the deck and unceremoniously held out a disposable glass of what seemed to be aggressively lukewarm stimulative elixir. When I shook my head to politely decline, she simply stabbed a finger toward the ticket stub poking out of my jacket pocket (which displayed its upgrade stamp), then wordlessly thrust the glass into my hand.

"Thank you," I intoned with sincerity.

Though I was not particularly pleased with this new liquid burden, I was even less pleased when she promptly knelt down and pulled my boots off to begin massaging my feet. I murmured a hesitant demurral, but quickly gave up in the face of her indifference, especially since the ministrations of her hands were *much* more effective than her demeanor might have suggested, and I was still feeling quite tense and wounded from my visit to Palace Equinox. However, when she raised herself several minutes later to begin unbuckling my trousers, I insisted on demurring rather more vigorously, and she stabbed at my ticket several times with increasing confusion before shrugging and walking away—under a much springier step than she had arrived with, I couldn't help but notice.

Such, apparently, was the full extent of what superlative amenities #9,800 in cash yielded on this particular line, but by then I considered it an investment well-made, given the circumstantial dividends in solitude for the rest of the journey.

Glory to the Returns.

I settled back to watch the sparkling lights of the districts dwindle away beneath me, and had nearly fallen asleep by the time we passed through the mid-bounds of the ionosphere some 15 minutes later—thankfully having kept the glass of elixir somehow upright in my hands.

I checked my chronometer, which indicated we were just about to enter the time period when scouts begin to appear. Fortunately, despite its obvious state of neglect, this shuttle still contained a few cupboards stuffed with augmented viewing goggles leftover from its touristing days, and once I'd wiped one as clean as it could be, I activated its mapping overlay and began scanning the swiftly darkening sky outside the windows. The deck's interior lighting conveniently dimmed in turn (providing a multi-purpose ambiance, in recent hindsight).

For several minutes nothing was visible save the sentry vessels of Alpha Corps, already staged around the system in anticipation of the scouts' arrival. I'd just lowered the goggles to rest my arms when I happened to catch a lucky glimpse of the telltale micro-burst of bright light that announces the arrival of a Fleet Eternal vessel.

Even with the aid of the mapping overlay, it still took a few moments to pinpoint the ship among the vastness surrounding it. According to the overlay scale it was roughly the size of an individual short-range hopper, but of course, like all Fleet Eternal's widely diverse designs, it looked nothing like a human vessel. From what I could tell, it appeared to consist of a fairly small spherical core which was studded with an alarming density of spiky protrusions and unidentifiable pylons. It was rotating slowly around several axes at once, but otherwise showed no sign of activity.

I'm sure you've seen as many halfhearted primetime reports as I have on the scouting engagements (given their intensely routine nature and status as a reliable source of late-month journalistic fluff), so you're familiar with their general tempo and flow. A few hundred scouts show

     TINY PLANET FILLED WITH LIARS

up, scattered all around the system; Alpha Corps positions its sentries to present something like a (relatively) formidable defense while keeping a wide (and stationary) distance; then after 40-to-80 minutes, the scouts depart. A full incursion follows eight days later.

If you're a decade or two older than I am, you may remember first-hand the last time some puffed up Board member managed to convince the military to attempt an attack on the scouts, along with the extensive scandal that played out in the years afterward when the assault led to a predictable and pointless defeat-via-massacre, which was then followed by the regularly scheduled incursion eight days later—right on time and unchanged in strength.

So you can imagine my surprise when the map began showing Alpha Corps vessels *in motion*, seemingly on courses headed straight toward Fleet Eternal scouts. One squadron of corvettes appeared to be particularly intent on performing an attack run, and once I found them in the overlay they were easily tracked by eye, since they were spotlighted by Jupiter's light reflecting off their hulls—though from my perspective the star was well under the horizon by then. I watched intently, holding my breath, fully anticipating an inexplicable repeat of that historical butchery, when the corvette squad suddenly veered away moments before crossing the engagement line.

I personally witnessed no less than twenty such feinting runs over the course of my journey, and just after my shuttle began its descent back into the atmosphere, Fleet Eternal's scouts departed without further event.

The glass of stimulative elixir (noxious as anticipated) had long since disappeared down my throat—which was good, because I needed the energy to curse upon discovering that the memory port on the goggles was empty.

Having rushed home to view what I was certain would be a chaotic evening report spurred by anchors trying to grapple with why and what had just happened, I found instead that not a single program even mentioned that a scouting engagement had occurred.

Bartimus Caldwell
[redacted]

[Bartimus Caldwell]

I wouldn't say that, sir.

[Interviewer]

(sighs)

I know you wouldn't, Bartimus. And I'm sure you genuinely *don't* care, but I do. You'd think 2,000 Class A shares would open the *possibility* of a short-notice reservation, and you'd be wrong. I sincerely, deeply apologize for these conditions. I am mortified.

[Bartimus Caldwell]

It's not even that bad, sir. I know the lobby floor was pretty ... grimy ... but I had a peek inside the dining room on my way up, they had a table filled with pastries and everything. Honestly, I'd be perfectly happy to stay here ... if I were.

[Interviewer]

Yes, yes, I know you're not bothered.

[B.C.]

I'm really not, sir.

[Int.]

And for fucking godsake Bartimus, stop calling me sir.

[B.C.]

Yes—yes, okay.

...

I mean, look, the towels are embroidered with their [redacted] logo and everything, they can't be *that* budget.

[Int.]

God, no, don't say the name, Bartimus. I'll just delete it from the transcripts anyway. Please, save me the trouble, I beg of you.

[B.C.]

... okay. You seem ... are you alright? Maybe sit down, take a breath.

(laughs)

[Int.]

Let's just get to my questions.

[B.C.]

Yes, sir.

[Int.]

(sighs)

...

The ... uh ... the scouting engagement, two days ago.

[B.C.]

Yes, like I tried to say earlier—

[Int.]

Please, Bart, let me finish the question.

...

The scouting engagement. Explain to me what happens in the Alpha Vector Operations Center during such an event.

   TINY PLANET FILLED WITH LIARS

[B.C.]

Okay, but—

[Int.]

Just walk me through from the start of an engagement. You're in AVOC. What happens?

[B.C.]

...

Okay. Well ... I don't mind scouting engagement days, actually, because we're not required to show up until 1500, except for the tactical analysts.

[Int.]

Why do they need to arrive earlier?

[B.C.]

They calculate the most likely deployments of the incoming scouts, based on a rolling analysis incorporating positional parameters and other metrics from the last twelve months of engagements.

[Int.]

I see. Continue.

[B.C.]

So, anyway, the rest of us on the balcony show up by 1500, and the OC is fully staffed by 1700.

[Int.]

Three hours before the engagement window.

[B.C.]

Correct, sir.

...

Uh, from there the rest of us mostly sit around bored until the first contact is announced.

[Int.]

What is your sub-unit's duty during the engagement itself?

[B.C.]

We're really only there to give an alert in the rare case when the tac analysts are incorrect and a scout arrives where it wasn't expected, so the sentries can redeploy at a safe distance, if necessary. Otherwise we mostly just watch, not that there's anything interesting to see ... usually.

[Int.]

Once contact is announced, what happens then?

[B.C.]

Well, the balcony starts rotating so the tac analysts can get a good view of the RAAWR display in all quadrants.

[Int.]

Wait, the *balcony* rotates, Bartimus? Around the entire room?

[B.C.]

Correct.

[Int.]

Why doesn't the RAAWR display rotate instead? Seems a lot easier.

[B.C.]

Um ... I'm not completely sure. But I do know that the bidding war for the contract to install the rotating balcony mechanism was very competitive.

[Int.]

Ah. Of course.

...

Okay, continue. The balcony rotates.

[B.C.]

Yes, the balcony rotates and the tac analysts confirm positioning, with Scry support if necessary.

[Int.]

And then, once the engagement is in full throe?

[B.C.]

Well, that's really it, really. We just sit there, and the scouts just sit there, and the sentries just sit there, and then forty-to-eighty minutes later, they disappear, we verify the AAR, and we all go home.

[Int.]

Okay, right. So, obviously, that is the point at which matters diverged during *this* particular engagement, so walk me through what happened *this* time instead.

[B.C.]

Well, that's what I was trying to explain before. I wasn't there.

[Int.]

What? Were you off-duty? Were you sick?

[B.C.]

No, sir. *None* of us were there.

[Int.]

None of whom?

[B.C.]

Uh, none of ... nobody. No analysts, no Scries, no ... nothing.

[Int.]

(impatient snort)
I don't understand.

[B.C.]

Um ... we received a command override at noon that day, fur-loughing all personnel Grade XV and below until the following morning.

[Int.]

What? You're telling me nobody but the top five Grades were even present in the room during this engagement?

[B.C.]

Yes.

...

Well, and the Overseeing Board members.

[Int.]

...

Jupiter above.

...

Fuck.

[B.C.]

Sir?

[Int.]

Wait, how could the operation even have proceeded without tacti-cal or sensor support?

[B.C.]

Well ... I guess ... the sentry pilots must have been given pre-briefed orders and been allowed to operate on their own recogni-zance during the engagement, using on-board acquisitions systems to ... uh ... monitor the scouts.

...

Seems pointlessly risky to me, if I'm being honest. But it could've been done.

     TINY PLANET FILLED WITH LIARS

[Int.]

I—

...

Jupiter above.

10

Lieutenant (Junior Grade)
MaeLi Meszaros

*4th Division "Stalwart" HQ,
Administrative Annex, Conference Room 2T*

[Interviewer]

I am recording.

[MaeLi Meszaros]

Okay.

[Interviewer]

Say again what you just told me.

[MaeLi Meszaros]

Say what?

[Int.]

(sighs)

…

I informed your command that, pursuant to the rights and responsibilities of my Cert, I required an interview with no less than five senior officers in your unit, limited to those who directly participated in the scouting engagement of end February and were present on the command deck of one of Alpha Corps' deployed sentry vessels during said engagement.

…

So I ask again, whom will I be speaking with after I've finished speaking with you?

[M.M.]

I am the only unit member authorized to meet with you.

[Int.]

State your name and rank.

[M.M.]

Lieutenant Junior Grade MaeLi Meszaros.

[Int.]

Are you a senior officer?

[M.M.]

No, I am not.

[Int.]

Will I be meeting any senior officers with your unit today?

[M.M.]

I am the only unit member authorized to meet with you.

[Int.]

...

Lieutenant, is it your unit's intention to violate the rights duly accorded me by my Intellectual Dominion Cert, eye-dee-see-four-three-dot-nine-nine-one-dot-ex-eye-dot-three, perpetua, and two additionally related Certs, as filed with, and posted by, the Central Office of Applied Thought, whose purview and authority supersedes that of every individual in this building?

[M.M.]

I am not privy to command-level decisions and cannot speak to such.

     TINY PLANET FILLED WITH LIARS

[Int.]

Lieutenant, have you been sent here to frustrate my attempts to gain more information, further, make it clear that your unit believes it can operate extra-legally in this matter, and finally, threaten my ability to properly perform the duties attendant to this Cert?

[M.M.]

I am not privy to command-level decisions and cannot speak to such.

[Int.]

And if I told you that refusal to comply with the rights of my Cert and answer my questions to the best of your ability opens you to prosecution for violating the mandates of the Central Office of Applied Thought, punishable by up to twenty years incarceration, as outlined in System-Unified-Code-dot-three-two-nine, Alpha, amended, what might your response be?

[M.M.]

I am an enlisted officer of 4th Division, "Stalwart," and all legal considerations, matters, and proceedings must go through the Inspector General of 4th Division, "Stalwart."

[Int.]

(sighs)

...

...

Lieutenant, were you given instructions as to how you should answer my questions?

[M.M.]

Yes.

[Int.]

Lieutenant, who gave you said instructions?

[M.M.]

I am not privy to command-level decisions and cannot speak to such.

[Int.]

Whose mouth did the words instructing you regarding this meeting come out of? Or whose desk was the memo sent from?

...

What *name* was attached to *any* communication you received regarding this matter?

[M.M.]

I am not authorized to discuss privileged communications.

[Int.]

Under whose authority?

[M.M.]

I am an enlisted officer of 4th Division, "Stalwart," and all legal considerations, matters, and proceedings must go through the Inspector General of 4th Division, "Stalwart."

[Int.]

...

...

Lieutenant.

[M.M.]

Yes.

   TINY PLANET FILLED WITH LIARS

[Int.]

Were you even one of those service members who was stationed or otherwise on-duty during the scouting engagement of end February?

[M.M.]

I was not.

[Int.]

I see.

...

We're done here. Get out.

[M.M.]

With respect, if you are concluding your business here, it is you who must leave. I will inform the security detail that you are ready to depart. Good day.

11

The Interviewer

Etc. and Rue Boulevard, Industrial District 12

IF YOU'VE ever suffered the misfortune of requiring assistance from the network cartel's user support department, you will *most certainly* understand the specific type of impotent rage with which I walked away from the looming edifice of 4th HQ, after being escorted out by a *full* security detail.

The undeniable and indefensible insubordination that the 4th Division had chosen to express to me, via its Junior Grade Lieutenant of indeterminate assignment, made it immediately clear that this calculated display had occurred on Board orders. Particularly since such insubordination was, by definition, also conveyed to the Central Office of Applied Thought, whose authority I obviously wielded by purchasing the Cert.

Vanderbilt. By then I had little doubt that he held a central role in whatever was occurring, but most especially with regards to Meszaros and her unit. The particular dehumanizing brazenness of the whole performance would have made that clear, even if the larger circumstantial context had not already done so.

It was not lost on me that this meant Vanderbilt had been showing his penis to me in the tertiary drawing room during the very same evening when he knew his scouting scheme—whatever it might be—was about to play out.

Accordingly, I knew—even as I'd filed it—that my writ of protest and notification of Cert breach in faith would go unanswered. Similarly, I knew that any attempts to follow up or expedite would be stonewalled with bricks gilded by a strain of legal privilege that can only be secured through wealth like Crowley Vanderbilt's. Nonetheless, I hope you understand me enough by now to know how *firmly* I'd slapped that protest submission form down on the desktop of some nameless COAT bureaucrat the very same afternoon, my eyes blazing with righteous fire as he wiped his nose with one hand and waved me away with a bored nod.

I'd briefly considered demanding an interview with top-Grade personnel in the Operations Center, but knew that Vanderbilt's influence would be just as strong there, thus pre-defeating the maneuver. On top of that, I was in no hurry to give Alpha Vector Defense the opportunity to reconsider my continued access to Bartimus, who had turned out to be *much* more useful to my task than I suspect they anticipated. I certainly didn't need them to find out that the man had been persuaded to actually answer my questions.

For all those reasons, I chose to thumb my chin at the military for the time being, and had willfully plummeted from the heights of the upper echelons to turn, instead, to one Hector Luis Deshpande, President Exemplar of the Third Street Amateur Astronomical Society—InDist 12's finest skyward observers—whom I was now scheduled to meet, the day after my pointless interview at 4th HQ, and four days before the March incursion.

Hector's coven of enthusiasts was at all times vigorously engaged in the scrying of the stars, with no less than fourteen separate telescopic installations in use around their little patch of the city. Further, they were banner members of the global Amateur Astronomical Society Federation, and so had access to a functionally limitless dataset spanning every

     TINY PLANET FILLED WITH LIARS

quadrant of the sky at any hour of the day. While every such instrument would, as a matter of course, be trained on heavenly bodies trillions of kilometers distant (or more), their mechanisms also happened to record orbital activity along the way. Though I had been necessarily vague when making initial contact, Hector seemed assured that he could provide what I required: A complete record of the movements of every Alpha Vector sentry during the engagement of end February, especially with respect to the positions of the various Fleet Eternal scouts at the time.

As I walked briskly to make our meeting at the appointed evening hour, I was internally engaged in a hypothetical struggle about the ethical considerations should Hector insist on compensation. Would paying him and his compatriots simply be an analogue to paying coterie access fees, since they (of course) were not coterie members themselves? Or, when paid to an unaffiliated source, would this amount to bribery that might theoretically impeach the integrity of the data for my purposes? I *could* hire them as contractors, but at great expense and even greater bother—especially if this would be our singular transaction, and not the start of an ongoing relationship.

Unfortunately I never came to a conclusion that evening, because as I was deep in thought on the matter and five blocks distant from the shuttle station that had delivered me to the district, the 15-centimeter nano-honed alloy utility blade (#28.99, retail) entered my body between the rear left sixth and seventh ribs, penetrating to the sixth and seventh thoracic vertebrae, while narrowly missing the renal artery issuing from my heart, and somehow threading its way through the meninges surrounding my spinal cord without nicking the cord itself, before some poor girl walking the other direction began shrieking in traumatized alarm and the assailant let go of the handle to sprint away, incidentally tilting the blade within me upward while doing so.

As my nose drifted toward the pavement with a rather ponderous grace, I realized that Madame Zhou had been quite correct. The indent sent to cut my heart out from behind had *not* checked my pockets for a Cert first.

Idiot.

/|\

If you've never had the pleasure, let me explain what it feels like to be stabbed in a mortal capacity. Penetration having been achieved, matters progress in three stages:

First, it is very, very cold. Next, it is very, very warm. Finally, it is very, very wet.

It is this latter sensation which holds the most weight in my dim memory of the minutes immediately following the assault—particularly as manifested by the distinct perception that I was slowly sinking into a boundless sea; which was likely driven by the swiftly rising pool of blood flowing from my multi-fractured face onto the pavement beneath— though I did not recognize the danger of drowning in my own fluids, being barely conscious at the time.

Fortunately for the mandates of posterity, the shrieking girl had been engaged in an animated conversation over her mobile receiver while walking, and though she did *not* avail herself of the device to call for emergency assistance, she did conveniently drop it within several meters of my body while stumbling back in gibbering terror. Equally conveniently, her conversation partner, for unknown reasons, vacated the call immediately but did not terminate it, thus providing a complete audio record of the event which I secured via Cert authority download some days later.

I will relay the contents of that call to you now.

For several minutes, the receiver picks up mostly indecipherable alarm and urgent conversation as more pedestrians become aware of my circumstance and, presumably, mill about aimlessly while waiting for somebody to do something. Fortunately, at some point during this period of general uselessness, someone does manage to call the emergency medical brigade, though I've never been able to discover who that productively-minded individual was.

During the interim, somebody with an undefined level of medical training feels comfortable enough to get near my body (and the receiver) to announce with authority, "We should probably try and stop the bleeding, ya think?"

Garbled conversation ensues for several moments, before somebody else proclaims (with a distinct air of panic in their voice), "I got just the thing!" followed by footsteps pounding out of range of the receiver.

Said footsteps pound back into range a short time later, followed by the first voice interjecting, "What the fuck is that? Why you got a god-damn BARREL full of it?"

The second voice says, "It's wholesale!"

The first voice: "Who cares?! You only supposed to brush a couple milliliters on, fuck you gonna do with a full—CAREFUL!"

It is at this point, in my understanding, that the owner of the second voice stumbles and dumps nearly an entire four-liter bottle (#724.99, wholesale) of ultra-bond liquid dermal bandaging onto my person, where it immediately cascades over most of my thighs and my entire back (including the knife handle protruding from it), gluing me quite securely to the cold pavement beneath.

"Holy shit!"

"Jupiter fuck!"

"Holy shit!"

"You idiot!"

"Holy shit!"

And so forth.

Fortunately, roughly 90 seconds into the next incidentally recorded conversation (in which a group of voices urgently tries to figure out why I'm bleeding so much from the face, and debates whether or not I'll suffocate if they start scooping nearly-cured liquid bandage off the ground to smear on my visage), the emergency medical brigade arrives.

"Get back!"

"Holy shit!"

"You fucking morons!"

"Get BACK!"

"Holy FUCKING shit!"

And so forth.

Soon one of the brigade says, "No, it's too late, look it's fully cured now," then calls, "BRING THE MELT BLADE!"

It is evident from the audio that, over the next several minutes, the emergency personnel strike a laudable balance between the acute necessity of getting my swiftly deflating bloodbag of a body into their craft, and the delicacy required to slice me free of my bandage cocoon first. Unfortunately, in their duress they don't notice that half a liter of the dermal liquid has worked its way underneath me and saturated through my clothing where the stomach meets ground, curing just as firmly as the rest.

The discordant howl which bursts out of my throat when they finally endeavor to heave me off the walkway is something I hope to never hear again, and I am exquisitely grateful to the budget audiophonics of the girl's receiver for distorting so many of the most disturbing frequencies. I am equally grateful for being too insensate to hold a firsthand memory of this abdominal flaying, particularly regarding the *internal* acoustics of how it must sound when one's own outer layer rips away.

   TINY PLANET FILLED WITH LIARS

I do not envy the poor sod who was tasked with scraping my epidermis off the pavement that night.

I apparently escape the pain by passing out completely with prompt mercy thereafter. One of the brigade members assumes the receiver is my own device and throws it onto the gurney with me as I'm loaded into their vessel, where it records some five minutes of impeccable emergency medical care, including the administration of top-class painkillers. In the midst of the journey, I rise again toward just enough consciousness to start wailing in horror upon notification that I'm being taken to a no-fee public hospital. This is followed by a brief scuffle punctuated by a few alarmed shouts, during which (I'm told) I literally throw my wallet at the pilot and manage to secure transport to a luxury facility instead; one whose services are a single increment below the palace-grade hospitals themselves.

Shortly afterward—just following an unknown medic's grumbled (and accurate) diagnosis: "rich asshole"—the girl's receiver runs through its last pre-paid minute and the call terminates.

12

The Interviewer

Jupiter Rising Sanatorium and Surgical LTD.,
Room 848, Care Level Epsilon Plus

MY STAY in Jupiter Rising was blessedly brief—though one would expect no less considering the truly absurd fee schedule I was subjected to. But I suppose just under #250 million is a small toll to pay for one's own life, at the end of the day.

Thanks to this price tag, I was up and walking (albeit quite stiffly) the very next morning, having spent the night heavily sedated while my body recovered from the billable hours laid upon it following my dramatic entrance to the emergency ward. I am told the near-palace-grade procedures used to repair my face, abdomen, and various components of the be-knifed internal cavity were a simple and prompt matter. However, the removal of my liquid bandaging shroud was a painstaking process that took nearly four hours on its own, and in itself amounted to roughly #forty-point-five million of my total bill.

All that outlay and I still continued to find flecks of synthetic dermal tissue on my person for several weeks afterward, so at least we know the bottle was worth the #725 charged by that unidentified wholesaler. Let us sincerely pray they never take a meeting with the hospital cartel's profit strategy auditors, or you may have just witnessed the dawn of a truly terrible age in tactical customer acquisition.

Still, given the alternative likelihood in an unpaid hospital—where I most probably would have spent several weeks in medically-induced somnolence before finally waking with a horror show of scar tissue to show for it—I was ultimately nothing but grateful for the outcome. Likewise, I remain grateful for the assailant's graceless motions while withdrawing their hand from the weapon, which tilted the flat side of the blade upward at the last moment, stretching the renal artery taut enough to move it away from the sharpened edge, where it otherwise would most probably have been sliced full upon my impact with the ground, thus ending our little story somewhat sooner than anticipated.

After waking, I took a thorough inventory of parts—all where they should be, though not quite all *as* they should be, given the interloping pale blooms of newly constructed skin, as yet untouched by Jupiter's light.

But soon I gave my mind over to considerations on the obvious question: Who had ordered this bungled assassination, and why?

Certainly the inanely audacious implementation of the attempt, made openly on a public street (along with the apparent pompous incompetence in choice of assassin) pointed squarely to Crowley Vanderbilt, whose potential motives needn't be explicated further. However, given her prescient warning of the assault, I admit to wondering whether Madame Zhou had ordered the attack herself. I could think of no logical reason why she might, but then on the other hand I had nothing but hope and a wounded sense of confidence betrayed to think that she would *not,* if such a motive were to arise. And, of course, instilling a false sense of budding camaraderie before an inevitable betrayal is a tactic not *unknown* to the denizens of Ruby, or to *any* proprietor of a business enterprise.

Thankfully, my fledgling worries were stifled fairly early on, as a lusciously expensive bouquet arrived with my breakfast, in which a small card, once opened, read:

Dear Idiot,

Told you so.

Bet your jacket ruined now.

See me when you better.

~Z

I am not too proud to admit that I endured a tearful moment at reading those words, so gracious in their own emblematic way.

Because my jacket was, indeed, thoroughly ruined.

/|\

Unfortunately, the warmer feelings attendant with that breakfast and Zhou's note were soon quashed as the night shift gave way to the day shift. The new nurse assigned to my suite gave one look at my chart and announced huffily (to the air in my general vicinity) that he *did not* work with someone with my "unique biology" before stomping out of the room.

One might wonder why such a decision would not have been conveyed more discretely to a supervisor out of earshot of any patient, but then, one in my position discovers early in life that for such a person the effrontery of openly stated bigotry is the entire point.

While the next nurse was quite apologetic and went out of her way to assure me that the opinions of the previous were not shared among the rest of staff, my mood was irretrievably spoiled by then, and I was counting the hours until my observation concluded and I would be discharged. Indeed, I very likely would have matched the previous insult with my own foot-stomping exit from the building Against Medical Advice, except I was curious to see my final bill as soon as possible, since I had not yet surveyed its brow-raising numbers.

Accordingly, I sent the nurse on her way with sincere politeness, so that I could better dedicate myself to the business of spending the day perched grumpily in bed while projecting gargoyle psychic animosity out into the general ether.

I'd been stabbed, then forked over millions for the privilege of being openly discriminated against, you know. Perhaps I deserved some sulking.

Later in the day, I recalled that I had incidentally been holding Madame Zhou's book within an internal pocket the previous evening, and found that it had been diligently placed inside the cellulose bag holding my personal belongings overnight. I retrieved it from same (while wiping a few more tears at the sight of the dermalized shreds at bag's bottom that had once been a jacket) and settled in to give it a skim. I quickly realized that I had been quite mistaken to ignore this book when it was first released some years ago, because it turns out the publisher's insistence on marketing it as another vapid personality-driven cooking tome was quite off the mark. While its pages did contain the odd recipe here and there, it was, in fact, primarily a meandering discourse on the ins-and-outs of wielding power in the Ruby District.

I won't recount the book here, since you can obviously go out and buy it this very moment—indeed, many of you have probably long since read it. However, one passage did catch my particular notice in an early chapter (printed here with all attendant rights and permissions), wherein Madame Zhou outlines the dynamics of running a sexual entertainment enterprise:

 Tiny Planet Filled With Liars

If you gonna run a House, you have to set the rules. Once they set, and once people know they exist, nobody got no excuses anymore, and no court in the world give a shit if you break them and get what's coming.

There's no need to tell scummers off the street about my rules, they make sure to know them before they even knock on my door. Plus everybody already knows the standards of Consent, and you can be damn sure povvers know they'll spend years in prison for violating them.

So, in almost 40 years here, I don't remember *one* time I had to throw some scummer pleb out the door for sniffing where they not given permission, no matter how drunk they get. Being too loud, or too cheap, or too sloppy even for me, then sure, boot to ass. But never for NonCon bullshit. No way.

But it's barely been a week since last time I had to put a crew of security babysitters around some Board member who needs to be minded like dog off leash just to behave decent.

This is the problem when you build class of people who exist outside the rules rest of us play by. They become monsters. And monsters can't just *live*, they think they gotta prove to you that you can't control them, because they better than you, even in your own House.

Lucky I employ big people for security, teach rules quick when some new whelp strut in. I might not be allowed to throw them out like plebs, but Betsy especially likes slapping Board dogs around to send message, and her hand bigger than my face.

One time I see her squeeze unopened bottle of wine in one fist until it bust all over Board punk's head when he keep touching without asking. Then she lean in close and tells him very nicely go back to palace so maid can do laundry before it's too late. She had diamond bit hidden between fingers, but punk too stupid to notice, think she can crush his head in one hand too. Nearly pissed himself on way out. Very funny.

Later punk try to sue me, I counter-sue and make his mommy pay me #40mil for wasting time. Very funny.

I encourage reminders that nobody gets to live outside the world when they guests in my House, no matter how much better they are than rest of us. I encourage you to do same in *your* House.

    TINY PLANET FILLED WITH LIARS

13

The Interviewer

BARTIMUS HAD come to visit me in the hospital shortly before my discharge, which was fortunate, because by then I had discovered that my previous up-and-at-'em spunk had been largely an adrenaline-fueled illusion—and that my body was, indeed, as exhausted as one might expect after being stabbed, glued, and rebuilt in the course of a single night. Receiving the bill predictably amplified this state.

For that reason, I accepted the hospital's suggestion of utilizing an ambulatory glider (source of a #600,000 appended surcharge, I would later discover), and also quickly accepted Bart's gracious offer to push me home in it. I can only imagine the irritation and further exhaustion that might have resulted from trying to navigate the glider myself through tight shuttle aisleways and steep embarkation ramps. (Even in straits like this, I avoid the taxi cartel entirely after enduring a terminal velocity "incident" in the upper atmosphere some years ago).

I mentioned to Bartimus that I was worried about being recovered in time for my appointment with the March incursion three days hence, and was considering skipping it entirely, given the wasted effort I'd just endured at 4th HQ. But upon hearing that I had been invited to view this latest round of events from the command bridge of 2nd Division's Prime Flagship, Bart urged me to keep the appointment, and assured me that they were "good types" whose assistance I would benefit from. I neglected to cite my *extremely* mixed feelings about embarking upon combat vessels to him, and simply took the advice to heart instead.

Shortly after ordering a bit of dinner up to the penthouse, I received a communique from the Constabulary notifying me that no evidence, genetic or otherwise, had been discovered on the knife itself. Similarly, all surveillance devices near the premises in question were either trained elsewhere or non-functional at the time, and no pedestrians who'd been questioned as potential witnesses could recall enough information to begin identifying the assailant.

Bartimus erupted in indignation at this failure, but while I *was* taken aback at the uniformity of the investigation's impotence, I realized I wasn't entirely surprised by it. Even I, by that point, had begun to understand the realities of the levers being pulled by very expensive hands when it came to my inquiry into the incursions.

Looking with hindsight, I doubt the authorities had even bothered attempting meta-investigatory steps like cross-referencing all surveillance within the region to assemble a census of those in the area at the time. But I'm glad that I was too tired by then to launch into an immediate flurry of follow-ups; both because I'm not actually a supporter of that type of meta-surveillance on ethical grounds, and because it would have given even more calendar space to an event whose entire purpose was to distract and dissuade me from my real task. Granted, such dissuasion was intended to arrive *via death*, but now that I remained alive, I'm glad I was able to stay the course without diversion. Not least because allowing myself to shirk 2nd Division's invitation in favor of chasing down my own attempted murderer would have meant missing the event that ultimately cracked this case wide open—though I didn't realize such at the time.

But one way or another justice would be done, and I would ensure it was directed at the source of the violation, even if the assassin themselves went free.

Thoughts of headline-fueled vengeance were waylaid by the arrival of a truly exquisite broiled collops repast accompanied by a 30-year-old Neutron Core Reserve (#28,999.99/bottle), which Bartimus and I tucked into gladly.

However, the revelry (stiff, sore, and tired as it was) came to a swift end when I happened to notice a regional evening news report, muted in the other room until I reactivated its audio.

A reporter was holding a typical stand-n-thrust engagement from the sidewalk outside a Jupiter temple, feet planted on the ground in front of a camera, thrusting her recorder into the faces of passersby for quick questions and even quicker responses. I immediately gathered that the occasion was one which many temples undertook every few weeks, wherein supplicants came to pray for solutions to some problem or another before receiving a quick blessing from a priest. Such a pageant would have escaped my notice entirely if not for the fact that one of the supplicants shuffling patiently in line was Crowley Vanderbilt.

When it came to his turn in the reporter's recorder spotlight, he smiled sweetly at her and intoned somberly, "I've come to pray for a solution to the quadrant's violence. Why, just last night twenty-one stabbings were reported in the tri-district region alone. A tragedy."

"Thank you so much for taking time out of your busy schedule to pray for our plight, sir."

"*Any* time," Crowley said, before winking into the lens and moving on.

14

Madame Zhou

ZHOU HAD clearly been expecting me the next day, as the door attendant greeted me warmly and escorted me straight to the kitchen upon my arrival. The swinging doors parted ahead of her to reveal a burst of fragrant steam carrying the words: "FANCY JACKET—the Jupiter fuck you wearing?! Did Zhou hear wrong? You sure you didn't die?"

I couldn't help but squirm. "Yes, I know. I decided to take your advice and be a little less … obtrusive … given the lesson I just learned."

She laughed—the rolling bark. "Yes, okay, looking decent would for sure be obtrusive, you right."

I looked down at myself, aghast. "Really? I'm not very familiar with *retail* styling of late. It was a difficult shopping experience, I admit. I thought—"

She interrupted me with a wave of her arm, chuckling. "Don't worry, Zhou just joke with you—it only as hideous as you think it is. You always be Fancy Jacket of my heart, promise. Sit."

"Thank you," I said to both her and Nobu as he handed me a glass of the canister tea featured on Zhou's lunch menu.

"Yes, very thanks to Nobu, mmm tasty, now fuck off."

I had just reached out to pick up the beverage when Zhou stood and I was suddenly enveloped in an aggressively protective hug—which gave way without warning to a thunderously "friendly" clap on the back, eliciting an immediate and lingering groan fueled by my stiff muscles and insulted epidermis.

"Owww! Fuck! You know I had a knife there not hours ago, right? God*ammit*."

She laughed heartily. "Yes, good, but near-normal amount of ow, or alarming amount of ow?"

I rubbed my shoulder and narrowed my eyes. "I'm pretty fucking *alarmed*, Zhou." But, after a sigh, I had to admit, "Almost a normal amount."

"Good. They do good work then, you not looted any more than usual for 'lux clinic. NOBU, bring fucking soup for fancy jacket." She returned to her seat and lifted a finger as I opened my mouth to decline, then continued instructing Nobu while firmly holding my eye contact: "Use the strong broth for healing poor stupid rich body. Very, *very* stupid, so must be very, very strong."

I let my mouth close and nodded with grudging obedience, wincing as I sat back.

Zhou resumed eating the plate of proteined greens in front of her, eyes flinty, surveying me while she chewed. Upon swallowing, she pointed at me with her dining tongs and said, "So, you like walking down industrial streets alone at night."

"Uh. It was hardly alone, in fact it was moderately busy as I recall. Also, is 'like' the right word? I was there with a purpose, about to meet —"

"Who care who you meeting, you still be stupid rich asshole walking down unmonitored street completely alone. Idiot. You lucky Zhou not walking along and see you there herself or I'd stabby stab you first just for being so dumb."

   Tiny Planet Filled With Liars

I sighed and abandoned further interjection, instead focusing on the soup Nobu had set in front of me while Zhou held forth.

"What I just get done telling you?" she continued. "You dealing with people not intend to play by the rules. Including 'don't stab no one' rules, idiot. I never woulda let you walk out my door if I knew you so dumb don't even got a part-time guard." She lifted a bite to her mouth while shaking her head and muttering, "Can't believe nobody murder you before now just to prove point."

At this I had to rouse myself again, feeling stung by her whiplash antagonism even in the face of my clearly pitiful victimhood. "Come now, I'm not—I have to tell you I really object to this characterization of ... I'm not some Board heirling—" Then a sudden wave of righteous glee washed over me—the kind that swells ahead of a devastating point of rebuttal—and I nearly crowed, "Anyway, half of *them* don't even have protection either! I've seen them, splattered off their faces, stumbling down the street totally alone, completely safe! Crowley was even on the news last night, waiting in a temple line right on the avenue, not a guard in sight!" I sat back, only just stopping myself from crossing smug arms. Point struck, *indeed*.

Zhou slapped the table and burst into a long, rolling bark, before tilting her head back to call, "Jupiter shit, fucking—YOU HEAR THAT BOYS? CRACKED THE GODDAMN SECRET! MYSTERIES OF LIFE SOLVED, YOU ALL GET DAY OFF TO CELEBRATE—SIT THE *FUCK* DOWN PETRE OR I'LL SHOVE *ANOTHER* TUBER UP YOUR ASS."

She sucked in a deep preparatory breath before snapping her focus back toward me, and I knew I was in for it.

"Blessed fuck fancy fucking jacket, you really *are* idiot." Here she lapsed into a mocking tone, "Oh my dumb face not see guards so guard must not exist, ooooooh my jacket so *fucking* fancy it turn brain into diamond turd. You fuckin' shit glitter too? Brainless britchless *fool*. Lemme guess, you think just because you see gildeds stumbling around in public here in *Ruby*—where *everywhere* be swarmed by coterie thugs the second someone with Board rights gets bothered—you think they living that way out in the whole wide world too, totally unprotected? How the fuck you rinse your own filthy holes in the morning with a brain like that running the hands? Don't you need a fuckin' mirror just to *REMEMBER THEY THERE?* Eh?!"

She threw down her tongs, eyes a terrifying flash as she stabbed a finger at me. "You listen here fucker, you *got no right* being so blind no more. Those times you see Board anywhere *not* Ruby without a guard? That just mean you looking at someone with guards expensive enough to be *not seen,* you empty fucking sack. Next you be telling Zhou nobody gonna get fucked no more 'cause you not seen a dick on the street today so they musta all fell off and fuckin' vanished right? Don't exist if fancy jacket don't see it, right? Right?!? Like a fucking **CHILD**." She bellowed the last, then struck the table again in coda, sending our dishware into sharp retort.

I jumped in my seat, lips flapping soundlessly a few times before I croaked, "I—"

"No, you shut the fuck up. You not learned *shit* yet. Can't be trusted to keep your own self safe worth *shit*. Rich and *dumb*. I know you now, gonna walk fuck outta here and find whatever sec outfit got fanciest fucking lobby to throw your sad little cash at, just so they know how much percentage to add on top for *next* Board dog who sends an indent to their door with knife and bribe hour after you leave. *Idiot*."

My face grew hotter than the steaming soup could account for. I never would have visited a security sales office myself, of course; a part of my attention had already been thinking about which concierge service

   TINY PLANET FILLED WITH LIARS

I'd engage to administrate the hiring for me. But her prediction otherwise rang true.

My shame was clearly self-evident, because Zhou shook her head and sighed aggressively, then visibly let the fires of her rage subside.

She picked her dining tongs back up. "Jupiter above, fancy jacket. What I get myself into with you. Like a useless baby. Very tall fucking useless stupid baby."

She stashed the thought in an enormous mouthful of greens and chewed contemplatively while staring at me. I was only too happy to silently soothe my pride in the bowl of broth.

Thus we sat for some minutes, enveloped in steam and the cozy clatter of the kitchen working around us, until Zhou had nearly cleared her dish and lifted an arm to beckon toward the doors behind me.

"Fancy jacket, babysitter. Babysitter, fancy jacket."

Before I'd even had time to turn and see who Zhou was addressing, a wide-shouldered woman clad in muted (but conspicuously and usefully tailored) attire appeared at my side—so silently I hadn't even heard the swinging doors move.

She extended a hand toward me and said steadily, "Good afternoon, sir. My name is Mira, I'll be running your security team from this point forward."

"*Holy* shit," I blurted. And in the next breath, "Do NOT call me sir."

Zhou cackled.

15

*2nd Division "Bulwark" Command Prime
(Standing Rains Berth 2A), Deck 32,
Ward Room Beta Eight*

[Interviewer]

Thank you for meeting with me briefly, Rear Admiral. I know it's a busy morning for you, I sincerely appreciate the kind welcome.

[Jon Smythe]

Mmm. Indeed.

[Interviewer]

I thought—

[Jon Smythe]

I see I was right about you. I was pretty sure I recognized your name, but seeing the way you walked clinches it. Drill camp dies hard.

[Int.]

Oh, shit.

[J.S.]

(laughs)

[Int.]

Forgive my language, I apologize, it's been an eventful few days or I'd remember my decorum more ... actively.

[J.S.]

Don't worry about it. Being stabbed entitles a few curses.

[Int.]

That's what *I* said!
(chuckles)
But I thought I'd trained myself back out of that drilling gait years ago.

[J.S.]

Maybe down in the world, but you're falling back into it here on-board.

[Int.]

Strange, considering I was never even stationed to active deployment and generally avoided combat vessels at all costs, even during ... Well.

[J.S.]

Anyway, the youngest may not know who you are, but I certainly recognize you, as do a few others. It's a shame what command did to you back then.

[Int.]

Thank you.

[J.S.]

Though I suppose it feels like more recent history to you than to me, eh? Don't your lot age somewhat slower than the rest of us?

     Tiny Planet Filled With Liars

[Int.]

Let's—uh, let's move to the questions, I think. I don't want to take more of your time than is strictly necessary.

[J.S.]

Of course.

[Int.]

This first one is purely to satisfy my own curiosity. I must be honest, I gave serious thought to declining your invitation after my experience at 4th. What prompted you to extend it?

[J.S.]

4th.

[Int.]

(chuckles)

[J.S.]

(chuckles)

But genuinely. There's a reason they're the 4th. I'd heard about the reception you received, and it's unacceptable.

...

Now, we've all got our own classification levels to abide, to be sure —and solidarity among the corps and so on, but [REDACTED].

[Int.]

I see.

...

Well, I genuinely appreciate the hospitality. Though I can't say I'm thrilled to be here in *fact*, I am certainly thrilled to be here in function. Not least because, as you know, it's legally impossible for me to have conversations about the incursion of February in most other settings. At least not without an exhaustive amount of bother.

[J.S.]

Mmm.

[Int.]

Given the events of last month's incursion, are you at all concerned about today's engagement?

[J.S.]

...

...

Bulwark is the blood and bone of the Alpha Vector Defense Corps, we've run this mission and *only* this mission for nearly 60 consecutive years. We are a finely tuned machine with a standing battle plan that's been rehearsed many thousands of times over—and executed more than 150 times on top of that—to reach a level of peak operational efficiency unmatched in the known history of orbital warfare. Every conceivable opposition scenario is planned for with automatic contingencies in the hopper ready to deploy with a single phrase. We are ready, waiting, and capable.

[Int.]

...

But?

[J.S.]

But wouldn't *you* be, in my position?

16

INCURSION DAY.

After an early morning start, I traveled to the Standing Rains launch complex and boarded 2nd Division's Prime flagship about an hour before my meeting with Rear Admiral Smythe. In stark contrast to my visit to 4th HQ, I was warmly greeted and escorted immediately to a reception galley with attached viewing deck. Here I was left entirely unsupervised to refresh, relax, and prepare for the hours to come.

The disparity prompted me to think about what Zhou had said to me the day before, shortly after I'd met Mira for the first time.

/|\

Zhou had just handed her empty plate to Nobu and was sipping on the glass of canister tea he'd replaced it with. She swallowed and tilted her head with a hissed tut before saying, "Listen here fancy jacket, you know why you need babysitter just to stop your fool self from getting killed? You making too much goddamn noise."

I fiddled with my spoon in the emptied bowl before me. "Isn't that the point? Aren't I supposed to be making noise? Shining light where light won't shine?"

She tutted again. "Sure. But only when it's time, idiot. You like a child throwing tantrum. You need to be like child schemin' something *sneaky*." She dropped one hand below the table, hiding it from my view. "You be *quiet*. And you be quiet. And you be quiet." Her hand popped back into view and chopped the table with a rattling impact as she said, "And then suddenly, when it's *time*, you be very, VERY loud."

She sat back and crossed her arms. "You don't be loud from the start and get yourself slapped and sent to bed before you even done anything worth doing, idiot."

I gave a frustrated huff, but conceded immediately afterward. "Alright. I understand what you're saying. I do. But I *don't* understand how you expect me to implement it."

She waved her eyes and threw her hands up. "Work harder to find ALLIES, fool!" She pointed toward her own entrance while saying, "Friends invite you in *quietly*. Friends want to *help*. Enemies fight you about it every step the way and tell everyone they know to keep you out, too. Stupid."

She sat back, arms crossing again before concluding, "You so dumb you expect enemies to help you fight them 'cause you got fancy fuckin' paper. No. Find people help you be *quiet*."

I nodded, accepting my tutelage. "Well. As it happens, I'm meeting with 2nd tomorrow."

She snorted. "Yes, fine, good start, they'll do. Behave yourself, and *make friends*."

"What? Don't I always behave?"

She cackled and shooed me toward the swinging doors.

As I pushed them open, I caught a glimpse of Mira slipping into shadow near the foyer, before the madame called after me.

"Don't come back for a while, fancy jacket. Zhou sick of your stupid face. Don't you fuckin' *dare* make me have to see it under a shroud."

/|\

Standing at the Crystaleen viewing deck pane, I peered down to watch the launch personnel buzzing around far below me, their activities on the berthing pad assuming a notable urgency as we approached the final minutes before the command unit's departure window. The lush sub-tropical forest that carpets the broad bowl of the crater valley stretched into the distance, its canopy broken only by the dark bulks of other vessels looming above the trees—many of them from other divisions, or non-combat units not involved in the day's engagement.

I considered Mira again, who was somewhere down there now, awaiting my planetside return later that evening. Though I'd already known she was (of course) ex-military, she'd told me the bulk of her enlistment had been spent with the Mamluk Mercenary Corps, which obviously has almost no interaction with the rest of the world, since its activities are limited entirely to Gamma Vector. Nonetheless, she'd been warmly greeted by the deck chief when we arrived that morning—in fact, she seemed to be on familiar terms with nearly every member of the Command Prime embarkation crew.

She'd asked my leave to request permission to accompany me throughout the ship's day, but had warned that such permission would probably be denied by command as a matter of routine procedure. Accordingly, I was not surprised when she suddenly appeared beside me several minutes after our arrival to intone that my security team had been asked to disembark.

"I have no concerns, you'll be in untroubled hands," she'd said before we parted ways.

It's strange. I'd known her for less than two full days by that point, but felt an immediate swell of warm safety at her words. I'm willing to admit now that I first genuinely trusted 2nd Division to treat me well in *that* moment, long before I'd been formally received by a single member of its flag crew, based only on Mira's assurance. I suppose I ought to have been more skeptical that my trust in Zhou had ballooned so thoroughly that it was now transferring to total strangers just because they existed *near* her orbit—and barely a day after I'd considered the possibility that Zhou herself had tried to have me murdered ... but then again, every alliance requires a certain degree of blind confidence to stoke the new embers, doesn't it?

Indeed, by that point I'd already moved well beyond the threshold of entrusting my life in its entirety to Zhou and her charges. At the first opportunity, Mira had explained to me the parameters of the protective bubble that would encase me forevermore. She stressed that she would remain the only public face of that forbidding shell. She urged me to trust in its vigilance, but to make no attempt to identify the other personnel under her leadership, and instead operate as if she were my lone bodyguard.

But as it turns out, this aura of secrecy was short-lived. It is, perhaps predictably, very difficult not to notice when the same four people keep appearing in the near- and mid-vicinity around you, day after day. By the end of March I'd come to personally meet every other member of the team. Though they likely won't feature much in the balance of this tale for obvious reasons, know that they remained omnipresent from the day I'd met Mira. Jin is polite but nearly mute; Stann cheats at dynasty swap and every other card game in the world; Gazala and Taara, lovers of history both, sometimes sing antiquated trench duets from the Consolidation Campaigns, and have brought me to tears more than once with their harmonies.

They are all very good at what they do.

Those are not their names, but you get the gist. Such is life.

/|\

 Tiny Planet Filled With Liars

Shortly before the launch window (and just before I was due to meet R.Admiral Smythe for the first time), the galley doors opened with a *whuff* and I turned briefly to acknowledge a small work pod, which looked to be on maintenance inspection rounds. As I felt the first thrum of the liftoff engines caress my feet through the deck plating, I was startled by one of the pod members, who was suddenly standing beside me.

Beyond that initial surprise, I was curious to see that she'd apparently been allowed to hold her post even with a boisterous mass of hair fanning out from beneath her protective cover. The utility overall she was wearing indicated her pod had just been inside the shielded engine zones, and even a non-combatant like me could recall the hours of being screamed at by engineering trainers in drill school about the *strict strictures* of zone-based shipboard safety, including the dangers of uncontrolled hair/clothing/tools/pride being caught up in the machinery.

She glanced at me and inclined her head politely, but just as I was going to ask her about herself, one of the crater valley's morning squalls blew over the berth and we were instantly enveloped in a wall of sheeting water. In a flash, the clouds were sending soldiers down to stand over half the valley—long pillars of precipitation hanging beneath their scudding billows, brooding above the forest floor.

"Ah, good," she murmured before glancing my way again. "Have you stood the rains before?"

"Only once. And I was not in a position to observe at the time."

She smiled, then quietly sang a line from the old shanty: *"I stand on the rains ... to touch the sky ..."* The sibilants in her words brushed against the soft hiss of droplets pelting the viewing pane, and I felt my senses lensing themselves together, caught up in the all-consuming physicality of a towering building about to lift itself into the heavens.

Our feet grew numb with the mounting vibration in the deck plating. We felt the gathering thunder of the engines rolling down our sternums into the pelvis, and our torsos began swaying back and forth as the massive vessel rocked in its cradle.

I realized she was silently counting down. As her lips formed *three*, all sound dropped out of the room.

Our hearts scraped across our bones.

Jupiter's roar unloosed itself and the air went syrup with the deep cacophony of liftoff. A hand shot out reflexively to steady myself against the pane, though the grav modules made it largely unnecessary. Outside the window, the squadron of Command Prime escort cruisers had grown incandescent blue legs, along with several other units in the near distance, and I watched as they all began stepping into the air around us, buildings in their own right, alive now to climb the same icy fire holding our own behemoth up toward the sky.

As we left the ground behind, the heavy squall poured off and over the vessels, forming misty tendrils that quickly coalesced into hazy towers hanging beneath each ship when the downpour intensified, the structures ephemeral, but standing taller nonetheless—taller every moment as the ships ascended into the atmosphere. And taller still.

My throat caught and I felt my lips mutely forming the words.

I stand on the rains ...

17

Various, Incursion Active Complement

**2nd Division "Bulwark" Command Prime
(Alpha Vector), Deck 54,
Command Combat Information Center**

[Admiral]

Audible count.

[Tactical 1]

Contact window threshold in—

...

ten, nine, eight, seven, six, five, four, three, two, o—

[Scry 1](simultaneous)

Contact trace!

[Tactical 1](simultaneous)

Contact!

[Armaments 1](simultaneous)

Weapons contact!

[Armaments 2]

Engaged!

[Scry 1]

Confirm.

[Admiral]

Banker Six Eight go.

[Tactical 1]

Banker Six Eight RELAY!

[Scry 1]

Marker one, nominal.

[Admiral]

You see that?

[Rear Admiral]

Yes.

[Admiral]

Caster One Niner go.

[Tactical 1]

Caster One Niner RELAY!

[Admiral]

SitCheck.

[Scry 1]

Point zero zero zero five CHECK!

[Rear Admiral]

The fuck?

[Admiral]

I know.

[Scry 2]

Marker two—

...

...

  Tiny Planet Filled With Liars

[Rear Admiral]

Marker TWO!

[Scry 2]

Marker two nominal.

[Rear Admiral]

Right there.

[Admiral]

Yep.

[Rear Admiral]

Hit those MARKERS, Yeomen!

[Scry 1](simultaneous)

Aye.

[Scry 2](simultaneous)

Aye, sorry sir.

[audible explosion]

[shouts, various]

[Unknown](simultaneous)

Jupiter FUCK!

[Operations 1](simultaneous)

Impact!

[Scry 1]

Incoming!

[Rear Admiral]

Condition ALPHA!

[Operations 1](simultaneous)

Alpha AYE!

[Admiral](simultaneous)

SitCheck.

[Scry 1]

MARKER THREE, FAILURE!

[Scry 2]

Point zero zero FOUR CHECK!

[Admiral]

AXIAL ABORT BANKER CASTER LOVE GO.

[Tactical 1]

AXAB-BEE-SEE-EL RELAY!

[Admiral]

That fucking west quadrant.

[Rear Admiral]

Gotta be SHITTING ME, AGAIN? SITCHECK.

[Scry 1]

Point zero zero FIVE CHECK!

[Communications 1]

AVOC open main.

[Admiral]

Mute.

[Communications 1]

…

Sir?

[Admiral]

MUTE MAIN.

[Communications 1](simultaneous)

Aye. AVOC mute.

     TINY PLANET FILLED WITH LIARS

[Scry 1](simultaneous)

MARKER FOUR, FAILURE!

[Rear Admiral]

SITCHECK.

[Scry 1]

Point zero zero FIVE CHECK!

[Rear Admiral]

Holy shit.

[Admiral]

ABORT STATUS.

[Tactical 1]

Incomplete!

[Admiral]

ABORT CANCEL OVERRIDE DODDER DODDER THREE CONFIRM.

[Tactical 1](simultaneous)

ABORT CANCEL AYE!

[Communications 1](simultaneous)

ABORT CANCEL CONFIRM!

[Tactical 1]

Override Dodder Dodder Three—

...

Confirm.

[Rear Admiral]

SitCheck.

[Scry 1](simultaneous)

Marker five, NOMINAL.

[Scry 2](simultaneous)

Point zero zero seven CHECK!

[Admiral]

Alright.

[Rear Admiral]

Godammit. Nice job, though.

[Admiral]

Mm.

[Scry 1]

Marker six, nominal.

[Admiral]

Okay.

[Rear Admiral]

There we go. Downhill.

[Scry 1]

Marker seven, nominal.

[Rear Admiral]

Nearly.

[Admiral]

SitCheck.

[Scry 1](simultaneous)

Point zero zero nine, CHECK.

[Tactical 1](simultaneous)

CAP-SIX-SIX!

[shouts of alarm]

[Admiral](simultaneous)

Show me.

 Tiny Planet Filled With Liars

[Scry 1](simultaneous)

Confirm cap-six-six.

[Rear Admiral](simultaneous)

What? Where?

[Admiral](simultaneous)

Oh fuck, there.

[shouts of alarm]

[Scry 1]

Marker eight, COMPLETE.

[Tactical 1]

DisEn InPro—

...

Complete.

[escalating shouts of alarm]

[Rear Admiral]

Oh, no.

[Admiral]

That last blast will kick their stern arou—Jupiter above.

[Scry 1]

Stand down conditions. Board is clear.

[Tactical 1]

Confirm. Clear board.

[Operations 1]

(weeping)
Confirm.

[widespread shouting, screaming]

[Rear Admiral]

Oh my god.

[distorted rumbling]

...

...

...

[twenty-three seconds of recorded background silence.]

...

...

...

[Admiral]

Lockdown.

[Operations 1]

Lockdown aye.

[Admiral]

No. Every boat. All fleet.

[Communications 1]

Um—

[Admiral]

All fleet. Protocol Black. SAR exclusion.

...

Genetic authorization Kudaibergen fifth-second-fourth.

[Communications 1]

Aye.

...

[lockdown alarm bell]

[Communications 1]

All fleet, Command Prime, lockdown, lockdown, lockdown. Protocol Black. SAR exclusion.

...

GenAuth transmission—

...

Black confirmed. SAR exclusion confirmed.

[Admiral]

Stand down.

[Operations 1]

Stand down aye.

...

Confirmed. Stand down.

18

Admiral Seersa Kudaibergen,
Rear Admiral Jon Smythe

***2nd Division "Bulwark" Command Prime
(Alpha Vector), Deck 52, Command Ante-Suite***

[Seersa Kudaibergen]

No, wait. Hit that switch.

[Jon Smythe]

Yep.

[Seersa Kudaibergen]

Okay.

[Interviewer]

(muttering to self) Mind your fucking business, is what that.

[Jon Smythe]

I'm sorry?

[Interviewer]

Uh, nothing. Stray thought. What the fuck just happened out there?

[S.K.]

Louelen?

[J.S.]

Probably so. On it. Your launch key in the desk?

[S.K.]

Yes. [redacted] while you're over there, too.

...

You'll need to be leaving now.

[Int.]

I will? From *orbit*?

[S.K.]

Indeed. Have you got your gear? *All* your gear?

[Int.] (simultaneous)

I—yes. Yes ... yes, yes I do.

[J.S.] (simultaneous)

Lou—

...

Yes.

...

Mm-hmm. Got your kids under the umbrella?

...

Good. Take a stroll this way. A *quick* stroll.

[Int.]

Um. Should I be concerned, Admiral?

[S.K.]

Were you ever not?

[Int.]

...

Good point.

[J.S.]

Alright, Lou's on the way. ETA five.

[S.K.]

Mm.

[Int.]

Lou?

[S.K.]

You'll have plenty of time to introduce yourselves over there. We're walking.

[J.S.]

Aye.

[Int.]

I—oh, I see. Okay. Uh ...

[S.K.]

The door won't stay open long behind me.

[Int.]

Of course. But I—
(pants)
I have questions—

[S.K.]

And now you have five minutes. I apologize.

...

You can go ahead and turn that thing off.

[Int.]

But I'd pref—oh.

...

Of course.

19

Various

*2nd Division "Bulwark" Command Prime
(Alpha Vector) and Etc.*

AS WE crowded into the chute control booth, I caught a glimpse through the viewing pane of the paltry vessel occupying the catapult pad in the adjoining chamber. I blurted out, "You can't be serious. Is that thing even exo-atmospheric? Does it even have a goddamn engine?!"

I promptly began a therapeutic breathing technique and squeezed my hands, which had gone deathly cold ... pre-empting the black brush of vacuum's sinister kiss ...

Admiral Kudaibergen glanced at me from the side of her eye and stifled a smile. "That's some of the most expensive cladding alloy in the world right there. Four contractors had to collaborate to finish its development. That skip is much stronger than it looks. And yes, it's space-worthy."

My head was slowly shaking.

"In any case, you needn't worry, nobody'll be forcing you aboard," she finished reassuringly.

In the same moment, R.Admiral Smythe put one hand on the hip pocket of his uniform, leaned over the control array he'd been examining, and barked into the annunciator, "OUR GUEST IS NOW DEPARTING VIA ORBITAL SKIP."

My mouth dropped open and I choked on a therapeutic inhalation.

The Admiral snort-laughed and calmly lifted one crossed arm to hold her palm toward me. She said to Smythe, "Did you set the auto navigate?"

"Whoops," the R.Admiral replied.

After flipping a few switches and receiving an unintelligible acknowledgment in response to his barking, he fished a launch key out of the hip pocket and inserted it into the control board. The viewing pane briefly shuddered as the chamber was vented, and the skip disappeared down the chute tunnel a moment later, gone in the space of a pounding heartbeat.

My shoulders loosened in one last analgesic sigh.

The R.Admiral turned, grinning as he said, "Don't worry, everything's just fine! Nothing to worry about."

Next to me the Admiral, who'd suddenly begun rummaging through a nearby locker, turned back, holding somebody else's clothes.

"Here," she said, "put these on."

/|\

Reader, I don't mind sharing with you (as I shuffled along the corridor behind the flag crew, trying to avoid internal inspection from a stranger's insufficient inseam) that I had begun to doubt the R.Admiral's repetitive refrain: "Everything is fine!"

I also don't mind sharing that I detected a *distinct* flush of impishness in his expression when he abruptly slowed down then hip-checked me as we passed a group of new recruits, sending me stumbling into their ranks while he and the Admiral strode briskly onward. Before I could even finish my wild elbow's apologies, the clustered recruits were snapping into moderately trained attention and marching with urgency toward a shuttle gangway just ahead.

Trapped in the riptide, I craned my neck (with some desperation) to catch the R.Admiral's eye, but he and the Admiral seemed to be studiously disregarding me as they came to a halt in front of an elderly individual in Commander's insignia, who was standing next to the gangway.

"Louelen," the Admiral said warmly.

"Seersa, Jon," the Commander replied.

"Just a quick taxi run?" chirped the R.Admiral.

The Commander nodded, then the two of them clasped hands for a few moments—a very peculiar gesture for Admiralty and senior subordinate, no matter *how* friendly they are.

"Alright, good talk, Lou," the Admiral said.

"Yup," the Commander replied (nodding at Smythe as their hands parted) before spinning around to follow us down the gangway.

My attention was then monopolized by the frantic energy of the recruits surrounding me, who were not so much marching into the shuttle as they were fleeing. I came to understand that they'd been out on their virginal plebby run; a recruit's very first experience observing combat operations in the flesh. Doing so on the Prime Flagship meant they were very highly blooded indeed—likely even destined to lower tiers of the Board in many cases.

To say they were taking the day's events with some difficulty would be an understatement. Actual wailing broke out while we strapped ourselves into jumper seats, and such discourse continued to punctuate the short journey to our destination.

Not that I blamed them, necessarily. Particularly during the magnetized combat launch.

Though I did resent needing to wait my turn to empty my stomach into the docking lavatories upon our arrival.

/|\

As I bade Mira goodnight and watched her stolid shoulders disappear beyond my front door, exhaustion was ready to overtake me. But I could feel the weight of the day's events straining my skull, and was struck with a physical urge to offload my burden into a database.

Fortunately, Bart had taken it upon himself to rush to my suite directly following the Operation Center's own lockdown, and with his help I was able to complete my preliminary notes before dawn.

   TINY PLANET FILLED WITH LIARS

20

2nd Division "Bulwark" Command Prime (Alpha Vector), Deck 54, Command Combat Information Center

SMYTHE HAD concluded our initial interview with a leisurely tour of the CCIC, before introducing me to Admiral Kudaibergen—who, to my shock, turned out to be the "maintenance worker" who'd joined me at Standing Rains during ship's launch. What I'd taken as a work pod had obviously been a command inspection pod instead. Shit.

My mind raced in hindsight through the varying social crimes that might describe how inappropriate my behavior had been that morning, considering I'd unknowingly been introducing myself to an Admiral at the time—and my *host*, on top. What kind of impression must I have made?

Well. First, I hadn't recognized her to begin with, so that was a heinous sleight right out the chute. (I'm embarrassed to say I simply hadn't thought to glance at the photo section of her officer summary during my abbreviated preparation for the visit. I can only plead "recently stabbed" in my own defense.) Next, I'd observed her intently (and silently) several times, answered her single question with vague nonsense, then otherwise would have appeared to ignore her completely in favor of gawping out the window at the rain like a newly weaned infant. And finally ... I'd *never even offered* my name before we'd parted ways without another word. (My skin crawls to think of it again, even as I write this.)

Unforgivably rude.

But despite my infractions, the Admiral simply smiled graciously after Smythe's introduction and inclined her head toward me for the second time that day.

Her hair, now unrestrained by the work helmet she'd been wearing earlier, formed a nearly solid cone around her face, stretching just beyond the shoulders—a status symbol whose violation of Corps dress code was the *point*, obviously. Beneath the sculptured mane, her command uniform displayed characteristics in stitching and ornamentation making it clear that her blood drew directly from one of the most prominent Prime voting dynasties, though her personal demeanor contained none of the aggressively rude quirks common to that class.

I quickly came to see how her coiffure served as both mascot and command reinforcement for the entire battleroom. When standing atop the out-thrust platform of the bridge, Kudaibergen's head was like a conning scope, visible throughout the enormous chamber, symmetrically sloped hair spinning with mechanical precision from one point to the next as she shifted focus, decisively broadcasting the vector of her attention at any given moment. In the course of my vigils that day, I repeatedly observed varying service members on the CCIC floor twisting around at their stations to peer upward and get their eyes on the Admiral's person as she went about conducting command. Early on, such glances carried an air of pep-rallying and pride of position, but as events devolved, the crew had clearly started using her as a totem, and was drawing morale from the very sight of her heedful presence on the bridge.

During the engagement's fiery conclusion, from my vantage the CCIC floor would become a pool of glistening whites, as fully half the

 Tiny Planet Filled With Liars

eyes in the battleroom turned to stare with brimming urgency up at the Admiral, their heads backlit in pulsing ochre by secondary detonations in the distance; supplicants for a miracle that even she could no longer provide.

Jupiter above. My ignorant rudeness was among the least of the crimes committed that day. I swear it to you.

The calamity of that incursion was foregone. It did not happen by chance.

There are *culprits*.

Pay attention now, because I am about to flex the liberties of this Cert to their utmost end, and I would hate to destroy the rest of my career for nothing.

/|\

First: The room.

Though the Command Prime battleroom is ostensibly an iconic showpiece of the entire Dominion, military enthusiasts have long learned to be content with only sporadic glimpses into the ever-changing details of this CCIC, which only tends to make appearances in rarely up-dated stock publicity photographs. Classification levels are often trotted out as the excuse for this fact, but an unspoken truth is that drawing at-tention to the CCIC more often would only serve to highlight how an entire (non-classified, and markedly extravagant) viewing suite had been included in the original construction to host Overseeing Board during incursions. Leading, inevitably, to the follow-up realization that this amenity has remained empty of such luminaries in every engagement over the last 63 years, in favor of the subterranean confines of the Alpha Vector Operations Center. Indeed, it's been more than a generation since said luminaries have even bothered nodding to nebulous security con-cerns as reason for their repeated absences—these days the invitation is simply not extended to begin with. Instead, the suite is generally treated more as an altar to authority; safeguarding the knowledge that Overseeing members of the Board *could* visit during battle and be appropriately accommodated, were such a singular event to ever occur again. This solemn watch requires the expenditure of several billion in renovations every year, in order to keep accommodations in parity with current tastes.

When hearing that fact at the time, I could hear Bart's voice in my head, assuring me how vital the suite was to fleet morale.

Glory to the Returns.

In any case; said accommodations, their forward half fully enclosed in Crystaleen, were set inside the flat aft wall of the CCIC, against which rested the enormous globular canopy of the battleroom proper, with its fusion-hardened Yeverian Manufacturing epoxy shell arcing gracefully (and nearly invisibly) around the remaining 300 spherical degrees of view, affording an unmatched perspective on Alpha Corps lumbering into formation all around us.

In full, the battleroom was just under 16 decks in height, with entry limited to several lower decks with direct access to the CCIC floor, and decks 52 through 54, where the cyclic lifts for command and support crew egressed directly into the bridge complex itself.

The bridge complex consisted of several clusters of open cubicle spaces and other workstations near the flat wall, but the real commanding was done on the bridge proper, whose free-floating architectural design allowed its lengthy suspended walkway to lift the bridge platform into the spatial center of the chamber. Here a balcony walled semi-circle enclosed an arc of ten workstations for the senior staff, with ample floor space set behind for Admiralty to pace and bark.

I must say, standing directly on the bridge platform was an intense experience. Both vertiginous and fascinating, the perspective afforded by

   Tiny Planet Filled With Liars

its position near the center of the bubbled battleroom often tricked my brain into thinking I'd been cut loose to observe the engagement while floating freely in space, with the shimmering ink of stellar fabric surrounding me at every viewable angle.

As you've likely predicted, my mental budget for this heightened sensory illusion was limited, and once events proceeded apace, I quickly assumed the position I would occupy for the duration of the engagement, tucked into a nook between the port-most workstation and forward balcony wall. Here I could surreptitiously clutch the railing with a clawed fist while otherwise calmly observing the 400 service members on the CCIC floor, their workstations, arranged in neatly gridded formations, draping over the curve of the bubble below me.

/|\

Next: The introduction.

I had expected to be remanded to the VIP suite once the work of the day began. But to my surprise, the first thing Admiral Kudaibergen did after our (re-)introduction was to inquire whether I'd had any difficulty getting my recording equipment through security. Following my assurance that I had not, she nodded briskly and said she thought I'd find the most utility in joining them directly on the bridge during the incursion, despite the break in procedural and security protocols.

As you might imagine, I could not decline such an invitation. As you might also imagine, I dearly wanted to do so, especially since the VIP suite was both armored to excess and host to a recently auctioned sonic sculpture (on private tour at the time) which I was quite eager to examine in person. The piece was titled *"Forewarned"* and had sold for #2 billion (after an initial #4 billion mis-bid scandal was resolved). It had been touted as a deeply political expression by promoters. It consisted of a table-sized hologram which, when entered by a viewer, flung holographic words like "Incoming" and "Ouch" at the face, before simulating a slap via sonic air shaping. I assume my interest requires no further explanation.

Unfortunately, duty calls quite insistently when one has paid this much for it, and I never got the opportunity to see the VIP suite at all.

Glory to the Returns, I sigh.

/|\

Finally: The battle.

Because I had never been present during combat in *any* CCIC prior to that day, much less Command Prime's, I cannot tell you with certainty that the behavior I observed among the crew in the period leading to the engagement was ... unusual.

But with more than four hours to fill after introductions, I spent as much time wandering around the bridge complex on my own as I did trailing the Admiralty while they worked. During these unchaperoned moments, I repeatedly observed crew on the CCIC floor (gradually accumulating as their sub-units took station) coming together in small clusters of conversation—often quite animated ones. Indeed, this activity lingered on until the final minutes before the contact window threshold. In the last hour, it was clear that mid-ranking and supervising officers were feeling pressure to assert order, and sharp admonitions began ringing out with some regularity.

Though the heterogeneous make-up of Command Prime's crew—containing titular representatives from every division and unit in the fleet—does give the post a reputation as the gossip crossroads of the Corps, I am *quite* certain that incursion day is not the typical venue for such exchange.

But as I said, I am ignorant in the usual details of CCIC conduct, and I am assured by several sources that no notable issues were logged by personnel review that day.

In any case, the bright line of the contact threshold was known to all, and by the T-10 countdown I beheld nothing but an expanse of seated heads diligently at work beneath the bridge. The Admiralty returned to the command balcony following their tightly classified final briefing with five minutes left in the count, and that seemed to mark the moment when the entire battleroom steeled itself for imminent engagement.

A similar moment of abrupt transformation occurred with 60 seconds left in the count, when Admiral Kudaibergen and Rear Admiral Smythe concluded a murmured conference near the suspended walkway and strode forward to snap into a wholly new form.

While the two had already displayed the usual hand-in-hand familiarity that grows between all long-term command partnerships, their interaction took on a new paradigm of cohesion following this transformation, and remained in such state until the end of the incursion. In my own memories of the most chaotic and terrifying moments of that battle, it's difficult to break the Admiralty into separate people in the recollection ... they're like two pieces of a single organism, biological planets in mutual orbit; when they walk to opposite sides of the bridge I can almost see their facing edges start to blur, questing for the other, gravity pulling them inevitably to fall back to equilibrium at the middle of the balcony and convey some half-psychic understanding of that millisecond in time to one another, before spinning off again to issue orders and dart eyes around the battleroom, hunting for the next decision to be made ...

As the Admiral called for an audible count in the final moments, the Rear Admiral made sure to walk the arc of senior staff stations, offering a hand on shoulders and quick words to each post. While the Admiral's portion of their shared orbit was concerned with all that occurred *outside* the Yeverian canopy, Smythe's included all that happened inside, as well. This led to that dense web of interlocking commands that is intimately familiar to anybody with deployment experience, but utterly inscrutable to most civilian sensibilities. Though either half of the Admiralty might be giving orders to any of the same ten senior staffers in any single moment (all *without* the inefficiency of addressing a recipient by position or rank first), there was rarely any question about whether the order concerned fleet activity, shipboard activity, or other—or about who should respond, in those units with two senior staff represented on the balcony.

Likewise, Kudaibergen and Smythe had long since learned to seamlessly navigate the enmeshed routes of their own responsibilities across the 105.8-second span between stepping onto the platform and clearing the board that day. I often observed the Admiral paying close attention to some aspect of the battle, only to instantaneously (and usually wordlessly) hand cognitive responsibility for it off to Smythe when it became a matter for Command Prime or the rear escorts to attend to, or when something else simply became more important for her to care about instead.

All this was reinforced through the very verbiage and structure by which orders were given and received, as any recruit can tell you after 14 months of grueling oral protocol indoctrination. And all of it depended on contexts that had changed by the time they were even functionally understood by those tasked with formulating, conveying, and carrying out a response. Even the most highly trained brain can only react so quickly, after all.

Ultimately, as Smythe had mentioned to me earlier, it was purely the result of endless rehearsal, which was the *real* toil of this fleet; today was

     Tiny Planet Filled With Liars

but the public performance of a densely choreographed routine that had already been drilled into precise uniformity over tens of thousands of hours beforehand. It was stunning to behold in action, and utterly impossible to fully comprehend in real-time, much less analyze.

I could never have even attempted the task without a recorder present directly on that command balcony.

So.

When the first bright micro-burst of the incursion's arrival swept across the black canvas outside, my urge to hit the deck behind the balcony wall was overwhelming.

Before that impulse could fully map my motor neurons the surroundings had flashed into a solid mass of micro-illumination and by the time I'd blinked my way back to clarity several heartbeats later I was frozen in place by the spectacle unfolding all around me as my attention ratcheted from one event to the next in a desperate bid to *understand* before it was all too late.

Problems became evident in short order.

My eyes instinctually avoided the terror of Fleet Eternal's first full salvo, and locked instead onto the Admiralty. Large holographic displays had sprung up all around the globe of the CCIC, filling the airspace with tactical overlays and data assisters serving various purposes throughout the crew, with a number of command status readouts floating near the bridge itself. While the Admiral issued her first formation orders to the bulwarks, R.Admiral Smythe's gaze was fixed on one such status readout, monitoring the progression of reset casualties as they headed toward .01 percent.

For the civilians among us, allow me a moment to explain the course of battle as it is drilled into every single Alpha Corps recruit, per Standing Order III:

Each incursion is broken into two sets of four quarters each, comprising eight total progression markers to achieve reset. Rather than representing fixed values, these markers are automatically calculated on a rolling and relative basis from month to month based on past performances, in order to maximize Alpha Corps' ability to achieve reset with the minimum number of targets destroyed, in the least amount of time. Each half of the progression markers is respectively referred to as "uphill" and "downhill" by service members, and it is this basic operational topography that serves as lodestone to the entire Corps. No matter how complex (or simple) their specific task during the incursion, no matter how confusing the combat situation itself, every single individual understands the sole operational objective:

Climb the hill. Come down. Hit marker eight in 90 seconds or less.

"Marker one, nominal," called out the senior Scry.

But the Admiralty took no comfort from the milestone, with Kudaibergen, swinging by in her orbit, muttering, "You see that?"

"Yes," Smythe replied, having also noticed that they'd *barely* made the first marker in time—its display had just started to flash a yellow warning before the switchover to marker two. Somebody out there wasn't doing their job. Many somebodies.

The Admiral issued order C-19, instructing both flanks to slightly disperse their firing patterns for the next two markers, in an attempt to get back ahead of the progression rate by quickly picking off lower-value targets. She called for a situation check immediately afterward, instructing the Scries to swiftly perform manual confirmation of current progression calculations.

Scry 1 announced .0005 percent Fleet casualties, which indicated a rate no quicker than the first marker.

The Admiralty processed this fact accordingly.

"The fuck?"

 Tiny Planet Filled With Liars

"I know."

With Scry 1 occupied, Scry 2 automatically took over responsibility for the next marker, but began the announcement with a questioning lilt in their voice.

"Marker two ..."

Smythe stomped toward the Scrying stations to investigate the hesitation. "Marker TWO," he warned.

"Marker two nominal," Scry 2 finally concluded a moment later.

"Right there," Smythe remarked to Kudaibergen as they passed one another.

"Yep," she replied, glancing at the Scry station. Another marker threshold cleared just in time. Something was definitely wrong.

Next followed one of those performances of obtuse military discipline familiar to anybody who's served, in which reprimands are given to individuals whose responsibilities *include* a problem, but who are not the *cause* of that problem themselves.

"Hit those MARKERS, Yeomen!" Smythe growled as he came up behind the two Scries.

All involved in the pantomime understood that the Scries had no control (or authority) over whether or not the markers were achieved successfully, and that Scry 2 had hesitated in their announcement only because the automated marker calculations had lagged behind before squeaking through in the last moment. Nonetheless, Scries "owned" the markers here on the bridge, and Smythe was making it clear that he would tolerate no further verbal hiccups in the course of battle, whatever the marker's status.

Both Scries accordingly and immediately nodded with drilled diligence.

"Aye, sorry sir," Scry 2 hedged, just to be sure.

A detonation popped off somewhere in the superstructure below the CCIC decks, eliciting a chorus of surprised shouts around the battleroom. Command Prime was not accustomed to taking fire, being so far to the rear in the Corps formation.

Operations 1 called out, "Impact!"

In the same moment, Scry 1 alerted, "Incoming!"

"Condition ALPHA!" Smythe cried.

Operations 1 instantly acknowledged the order and conveyed it to Command Prime's combat units, instructing them to drop the command ship's usual stance of minimal armaments participation (intended to prevent the vessel's own weaponry from obscuring the view outside the Yeverian canopy) and switch to active point defense instead, including flak if necessary. The same order instructed the escort cruisers surrounding the Prime ship to fire freely on any targets in range and shift their screening formation as required to intercept incoming. *Keep command safe*. Muted bursts of defensive flak punctured local space for the duration of the engagement.

The Admiral had just called for a situation check when Scry 1 announced the beginning of disaster.

"MARKER THREE, FAILURE!" she shouted.

A heartbeat later Scry 2 provided the Admiral's situation check: .004 percent. A meaningful improvement over the previous rate of progression, but still dangerously behind schedule—and now officially late enough to trigger marker failure.

In a *successful* incursion reset, the Kill Rate traced a sharp upward curve over the course of battle, as the whittling down of defensive systems in those Fleet Eternal vessels nearest to the Corps amplified Time To Kill efficiency gains. But instead of accelerating, the Corps' TTK and KR curves had flat-lined over the last marker, which meant they were now actively falling behind.

Kudaibergen was shouting an order in response even as she strode toward the Scrying stations to confirm the situation. "AXIAL ABORT BANKER CASTER LOVE GO."

Tactical 1 replied immediately, "AXAB BCL RELAY!"

Alpha Corps' standard deployment formation is roughly ovoid in shape, with the rear-ward flank located "down" or "behind" toward the planet, the forward line and its numerous bulwarks directly ahead to form the main combat front of the fleet facing "up" into Alpha Vector, and left and right flanks capping either end, based on that skyward-facing orientation perspective. In practice, members of the military tend to use cardinal terms interchangeably with these more formalized designations—referring to the left flank as "west," right flank as "east," and forward and rear accordingly.

Kudaibergen's order had called for an axial abort, instructing both left and right flanks to compress the formation by swinging back relative to the longitudinal axis of the ovoid, with a hinge at the point where each flank merged with the forward line. Among the many results of such a maneuver, the required movements served to reduce the spacing between individual ships on the flanks, and so moderately compressed their fields of fire. Without yet understanding precisely why markers were failing (and since the previous order to *spread* firepower had achieved little), the Admiral hoped that this boost in massed firepower would overcome whatever insufficiency was occurring out there in the formation.

It did not.

"That fucking west quadrant," she remarked to Smythe, who seemed to be instantly enraged by the idea.

"Gotta be SHITTING ME, AGAIN? SITCHECK," he barked fiercely.

Point zero zero five. Barely progressed.

At that moment Communications 1 announced that the Alpha Vector Operations Center had opened a line and wished to speak with the Admiralty. "AVOC open main."

"Mute," Kudaibergen replied immediately.

The senior staffer was stunned. The mid-battle call from Overseeing Board in the OC was a long-established piece of posturing political nonsense. Operationally useless—even detrimental—but mandatory in every possible respect except the officially codified one.

But the Admiral had no time for bullshit that day, and so briskly reiterated, "MUTE MAIN."

"Aye," the staffer responded, struggling not to feel chastened. (After all, it was his only real task during most incursions, since all fleet orders were instantly transmitted through Operations and Tactical stations.) He lifted his chin stoically and confirmed, "AVOC mute."

Forty-seven seconds had passed since initial contact.

"MARKER FOUR, FAILURE!"

"SITCHECK," Smythe called immediately.

Point zero zero five. *Still.* They had not progressed at all during the entirety of marker four.

"Holy shit." Smythe's face took on an ashen hue.

"ABORT STATUS." Kudaibergen sped toward Tactical.

Incomplete. Thank Jupiter. There was still time to adjust.

"ABORT CANCEL OVERRIDE DODDER DODDER THREE CONFIRM."

Cancel the axial abort maneuver, with confirmation. Override with order DD3. Direct Drive firing, three Alpha Corps ships per target, chosen based on per-class calculations to minimize TTK.

Bring them down. Now!

In order to understand the impact of this order, it's necessary to understand how spaceborne combat actually functions in the mechanics—

 Tiny Planet Filled With Liars

which I know many of you will not. Fortunately, the concepts are straightforward:

Every ship in the fleet fights with projectile weapons (in the form of railguns and missilery) and energy armaments (in the form of laser emplacements, at least for the Corps fleet). Only those ships positioned nearest to the bulwark defensive line are consistently in range for widespread laser contact, while the rest of the fleet tends to rely on their projectiles. Though lasers may be used with impunity, every blast of a projectile weapon (or launch of a missile) imparts enough momentum to the firing vessel that it must be counteracted via reaction drives. Such drives, positioned around all angles of a combat ship, are individually and automatically triggered to negate the momentum of weapons firing on the opposite side of the vessel. In traditional combat, this allows a warship to engage targets at any angle without needing to adjust the ship's own heading first—but at a moderate cost in effective firepower. Notably, the largest railguns on any vessel with more tonnage than a cruiser tend to be locked into forward-facing engagement zones, along with requiring a specific low-rate firing pattern during active combat in order to maintain firing accuracy to either side, and to stay in formation overall.

The Admiral's order suspended these normal operations, and instructed each relevant vessel to point itself straight at a chosen target, slam the throttle levers up into the chocks, and hammer away with all forward-facing weapons at full tilt, throwing as much firepower as physically possible before falling back out of range.

The result transformed orderly ranks of warships into a riot of vessels popcorning backward in straight lines as their unrestrained forward weaponry quickly overwhelmed drive thrust. In standard formation this would have made at least a few collisions with the interior fleet inevitable, but because each flank had been mid-abort, their ships were able to coordinate orientation such that they could slip behind the rest of Alpha Corps instead. Still, it meant an immediate and irrecoverable loss of operability, making it a last ditch effort in all regards. If the Corps suddenly needed those flanks to fight for *any* other reason, they simply wouldn't be able to organize quickly enough. A universe of consequences could pile up in the hour it might take to collectively resume effective formation.

"SitCheck," Smythe said.

"Marker five, NOMINAL."

Point zero zero seven. They'd finally crested. Thoroughly downhill from here. At last.

The senior staff loosed its collectively held breath.

"Alright," Kudaibergen said blandly.

"Godammit," Smythe said while drifting toward her. Being forced to obliterate fleet cohesion was not an achievement they would celebrate. But the maneuver had been very effective, and brilliantly timed—even a moment later and the flanks would have moved too close to the main fleet for safe execution. "Nice job, though," he concluded.

"Mm," the Admiral replied, already intently focused on the progression of the next marker.

The battle, after all, was not yet over.

So.

I know what you're thinking now. I do. I have avoided it for this long because I am, in part, embarrassed to admit how little edification I can provide. How deep my failures in this regard truly delve. Yet, even still, you want me to turn my head, right this very sentence, right there on that bridge, to stop looking at the Admiralty or crew and instead tell you right here on this page what was happening outside the protective canopy. What that flank attack looked like in person. What operational orders looked like as they rippled into action across the Corps surrounding us. How I watched the ebb and flow of battle streaming before my very eyes, in every plasmatic, bursting, incandescent detail of all the holo-assisted real-time glory that the most expensive contractors in the UFD could provide, and which I had paid the fortunes of lifetimes to behold in the flesh myself, above all others that day, throughout that entire world hanging naked and small below us. Exclusive rights. Exclusive perspective. An exclusive privilege.

Yet I cannot. I am sorry.

I know that for some of you this will mark the betrayal of my most sacred duty in this matter: the obligation to *witness*. The obligation to perform *journalism*. To see with eyes of meat; to make truth out of electronic fact by firsthand account of the warm body on-scene; to force you to abandon skepticism in the face of primary testimony offering up enough viscera to strike you in your *guts*.

I will not.

You will learn to identify verified, documented, empirical fact *now*, or you will not. *Here*, or you will not. My non-classified records are by now publicly available on UFD nets, as you read this. I cannot save your lives *for* you, if you believe what I have presented (and will present) in this text is not yet enough to draw your heartfelt attention.

What's more, I fear that the very banality of conveying this experience in letters, or via news broadcast, undoes any attempt to understand the impact of Fleet Eternal's warfare in a meaningfully tangible sense.

Take those news reports (produced less frequently in recent years, given the current lack of need to gin up popular support for the military through spectacle of combat), which purport to offer fact, yet are shot with cameras whose lenses automatically adjust light levels to provide comfortable viewing for an audience safely ensconced at home. You watch such footage of Fleet Eternal's energy weaponry, and you think to yourself, "My that seems awfully bright, look how much those people have to squint, must be uncomfortable."

When Fleet's first full salvo was loosed at the start of the engagement, when I instinctively turned away to direct my gaze safely inside the battleroom, I still felt the buzz of its energy arrays caressing my body; spillover radiation from the arcing flares that were washing over the enormous shapes of the bulwarks 60 kilometers ahead on the front line, vaporizing millions of cubic meters of ablative ejection armor in an instant. When I turned back a few heartbeats too soon, the fading brilliance of those blows still seared my retinas, even with the Yeverian canopy's automatic photon buffering, and I took no succor from Command Prime's position deep inside the projectile monopoly zone, well beyond energy range. Not when Fleet still called to my very skin.

And now, at the very end of the incursion, when a corvette-equivalent-class Fleet Eternal vessel inexplicably found its way through the front line near the left flank just before the final marker should have been announced and began raining energy assaults on the lightly armored rear aspect of a bulwark, my untrained vision was so swamped by over-exposed afterimages that it took me a few moments to understand what was happening, and why horrified screams were suddenly drifting up from the CCIC floor.

"CAP-SIX-SIX!"

The Admiral sped toward Tactical and Scrying. "Show me."

"Confirm cap-six-six."

"What? Where?" the Rear Admiral said, staring out at the tactical overlays in the battleroom.

"Oh fuck, there," replied Kudaibergen, pointing at a Tactical station display.

All four eyes of the Admiralty snapped as one to the far distance, where the waving tendrils of the energy assault could just be glimpsed as a wobbling white dot—though crew below had already thrown enlarged optical projections of the event around the CCIC floor.

I watched one such projection as the bulwark began to convulse under each lick of the Fleet vessel's weaponry, the interior support structures of its ablative umbrella severed and buckling. Near the bulwark, a mammoth-class laser boat stationed behind the umbrella's southeast quarter was swinging around at phenomenal speeds, the ship's navigational engines clearly beyond capacity as it tried to bring its point defense emplacements into bearing. The algorithm declared marker eight completion the moment the boat managed to snap-fire a flurry of support lasers onto the Fleet vessel, sending it spinning out of control toward the Alpha Corps ship itself.

Tactical announced disengagement in progress, completed seconds later even as the bulwark began spouting gargantuan flares of plasma.

"Oh, no," Smythe said.

The laser boat's direct propulsion drive blazed behind it as the captain tried to avoid the disabled Fleet craft. A plasma flare from the bulwark reached out and caught the ship on the rear, just ahead of the drive cowling.

Kudaibergen leaned forward. "That last blast will kick their stern arou—Jupiter above."

The optical projections froze on a blurred image of the laser boat, enveloped in the impact explosion, the silhouette of its entire 400-meter length tumbling like a toy before a field of snowy white.

"Stand down conditions. Board is clear."

Screaming broke out again as a bright burst laid across the fleet, and a moment later the speeding shell of a hyper-fusion shockwave erupted from where the bulwark (and its ablation reactor) had been. Decorum in the battleroom became an instant shambles.

"Oh my god," Smythe said.

I could hear lieutenants on the floor bawling orders to brace for impact. However, the shockwave had dispersed enough to lose its sharp edge once the front arrived, and Command Prime simply rocked in the turbulence of its wake. The battleroom fell into silence once it passed, as a string of secondary detonations in the distance made it clear that other ships had not been so fortunate.

Kudaibergen was standing at the balcony railing now, staring across the kilometers to the carnage at her west quadrant. Her expression was unreadable, but the eyes shone.

"Lockdown."

     Tiny Planet Filled With Liars

Hector Luis Deshpande,
Bartimus Caldwell

*Third Street Amateur Astronomical Society,
Industrial District 12*

"GIMME THEM SLUTS, SCRIES, AND STARS!" crowed the well-weathered senior circuit technician, answering my question as she shuffled by, toolbox in hand, before exiting the foyer chortling.

"Ah," I nodded in thanks when she passed. That explained the enormous banner hanging crookedly against the far wall ("AAS GOT YOUR SSAS!!!"), as well as the bright yellow Consent Information plaque posted on the front door.

"Wait'll you see the fuck room," Hector said next to me. He grinned at my reaction.

"Really?" I replied, shooting a glance at Bartimus, who studiously avoided my eyes.

"Naw, just jokes," said Hector.

"Ah," I chuckled.

"You're not allowed. Members only, and orgy night is only once a month these days anyway. We mostly keep it up for tradition—should see the albums we got in a closet somewhere from the *founders'* parties, shit. Alright follow me!"

Bartimus chewed his lip but silently fell in beside me as we moved deeper into the headquarters of the Third Street Amateur Astronomical Society.

"So, how long have you and Bartimus known one another?" I asked pointedly.

"What ... ten? Twelve years? Eh, Caldwell?" Hector responded without turning his head.

"I think so," Bart said.

Hector came to a stop and looked over his shoulder as he waved his hand elaborately in front of a finger coded door. "Never woulda thought back then he'd end up military. We was plannin' the block party for second summer ... or did we have it first summer that year? Anyway, our old sexual screener retired and had to sell all her equipment. Lucky Caldy here was already—"

"In the neighborhood," Bart interrupted.

Hector looked between the two of us with deliberation, then grinned again. "Sure," he said. "In the neighborhood." A rascal spark flashed in his eyes before he turned back to push the door open and concluded, "Plus he had folks lined up to lip his dick all summer long so he was basically family already. Wasn't there an actual waiting list that first year, Caldy? Coulda sworn ya showed it to me once."

Now it was my turn to grin as Bartimus squirmed and shook his head before saying, "I don't remember."

"Strange, Bart didn't even mention that he was familiar with the Society when I scheduled the original visit."

Hector glanced back again. "Oh yeah? Why's that, *Bart*?"

Bartimus sheepishly mumbled, "Come on, Hec ... kiss and snitch ... haven't even been to a party for years," amid a variety of non-words while Hector and I shared a smirk.

   TINY PLANET FILLED WITH LIARS

I was surprised to see that we still had to pass through several more coded security barriers before reaching the observatory labs themselves. After all, it's been nearly 20 years since the last time a rumor about astronomical equipment being confiscated by the military swept the world, but obviously the starhunters continued to take the prospect seriously.

"Here we are! Home at last. Fuckin' beautiful, yeah?" Hector raised his arms to the ceiling high overhead.

My eyes could barely focus on the dense patterns formed by conduits, wires, and unknown paraphernalia which lined every spare centimeter of the converted gymnasium, above and below; save narrow footpaths marking rodent trails for the warren. Here and there faded paint still scratched its way over the few visible floorboards, indicating areas where students had once been put through morning martial drills. I realized with a start that those students had probably been drilling for the Consolidation Campaigns, given how long the AAS must have owned the building.

"Indeed," I finally replied to Hector, doing my best to ignore the omnipresent hum of magnetic shielding in the chamber.

"Third largest observatorium in the entire global Federation," Hector noted proudly as he led us along a path, "AND the only one with a Heoffniretz Autoscry still kickin' around."

"Holy shit," I said. "How old is it?"

Hector snorted. "Well, the benny-factor themselves was a-hundred-four when they donated it, and that was 90-some years ago." He looked back. "So. Old."

I nodded.

"'Course its analyzer wasn't worth shit even fresh off assembly, we just use it to speed up signal ident mostly."

"Makes sense."

"Imagine if they'd actually worked though, right?"

"Indeed."

Bartimus sighed wistfully. "Doubt they'd need me in the military."

Hector pulled up next to a cluster of workstations. "You got good timin', think Vemda just finished up the analysis for March, probably just about done compiling in her desk right now ... 'course we'd already got February's put together for ya a while back." His expression took on a gentle cast as he looked at me. "You'd never tell, by the by, glad to see it. Near had a heart attack myself when I heard why you never showed. You're not swelled or scarred or nothin', huh? Can't fuckin' believe the shit they do in those palace places. If only."

"Mmm," I responded.

"Anyhow, data don't rot, should find everythin' you need in there for February too, just fine."

"I sincerely hope so, and thank you. If you don't mind, could we take a look at the newest incursion data right now? Is that possible? I'd like Bartimus to scry something for me."

"Sure, no problem. Lemme grab it. HEY VEMDA YOU GO TO DINNER YET? ... VEM?"

As Hector set off in search of the data, I turned to Bart knowingly. "Fuck room, huh?"

"Mostly just snacks and drinks," he mumbled before leaning in to examine a particularly interesting conduit.

"So I've been told."

"No, really. You know Eleanor—back in the foyer—her and her husband Chidi even do a mini-waffles stand on the stage, next to the band. They've been doing it for 40 years or something, don't even bother getting naked anymore usually, they're that busy cooking. Real dedicated. They're almost the best waffles I've ever had, too. Every year I can't wait until multiberries are in season, Chidi soaks—"

   TINY PLANET FILLED WITH LIARS

He abruptly looked up from the conduit. "Uh, *couldn't* wait ... for the berries. Back then. I meant. I don't even live in this district anymore ... but you know that already."

"Bart, shut up."

"Yep."

/|\

"Oh wow, yeah. I think your suspicion is correct. That's definitely a DAP." Bartimus opened his eyes, hands still splayed over the sensor desk. Upon Hector's bemused snort he continued, "Sorry. Deviant Approach Pattern, that is. For sure. Look, right here, this corvette veers and is barely a kilometer off the skip's trajectory. Even if they had a reason to be in that slot—which I can't think why they would, especially since you were all supposed to be Protocol Black right then—there's *no* reason for them to go crossing a dozen lanes to get closer. Look—put the overlay up, Hec ... right there."

I watched the maneuver he had flagged playing out: a squadron of at least a dozen ships, one of which broke off and nearly intercepted the auto-navigated orbital skip before holding position at a slight distance instead. I said, "No reason except ..."

"Except a local STS sensor sweep," Bart finished.

"Woof, Caldy. That's some big sniff for such a tiny bite." Hector raised his eyes from the display and looked at me. "You remember bein' particularly smelly that day?"

I sighed. "No. Especially since I wasn't actually on that skip, remember. Though I guess that's what the ship-to-ship sweep would have informed ... them." I shook my head. "I didn't even think about the rest of the fleet, any worries I had were about 2nd, and I dropped my guard with them right away. I never considered the other divisions to be relevant to my personal security during the incursion. Not while under the Admiral's umbrella. Clearly I should have." I looked down at the display. "Because ... the only possible way *they* could have suspected I was there to begin with ... would be if they were already monitoring Command Prime's local launch channels and heard Smythe say a 'guest' was onboard when the orbital skip set off back to the planet."

Bartimus raised his eyebrows. "Off reg."

"Yes."

"*Very* off reg. They're encrypted, you'd have to avoid getting logged, even—" He looked down again, his head shaking slightly. "I don't know ... that's really hard to believe."

"What's to believe, Bart? You're looking right at it, even if we don't understand what it means yet."

Hector nodded. "Fact. That's a fly-by, friend. Clear as crystal. You got somethin' plausible hidin' in ya'pockets instead?"

Bart shook his head. "I guess not."

"Right. Although ... I mean, don't wanna intrude on official business, but even as I run my mouth I'm startin'a think you two're ignoring a second scenario might be plausible."

I looked at Hector in surprise. "Go ahead."

"Seems like if those ribbon racks was advertisin' you as bait on an empty skip ... wouldn't that mean they were *expecting* someone to consider havin' a bite? Or even ... hm. Don't gotta bother with an outside channel 'crypt if you're not listenin' from *out*side. Right?"

I felt Bartimus take a deep breath.

I nodded.

"Okay," I said. "You're right. I concede that's a possibility. I admit to having the same thought before, myself."

I took a breath and squared my shoulders. "But we'll worry about who knew what, how, and when ... later. Let's see if we can confirm ex-

    Tiny Planet Filled With Liars

actly what those ships wanted with me in the first place, and it'll probably start answering the other questions too. What unit is that?"

Bartimus cleared the desk overlay. "Well, I was only able to spot Command Prime to find the skip launch because it's so far in the rear and easy to pick out. But there's no way to ID this other group using just the dataset, we'll need something to cross-reference with in order to figure out who's who—unless you have visual data on these coords that's not in the package for some reason?" He looked up at Hector, and nodded when the man shook his head in response. "Right, so instead we'll just follow their route back to the start and hopefully we'll be able to tell what unit they were positioned with in the standard formation, before they broke lockdown. It's probably some kind of light screen sub-unit, this largest one here can't be any bigger than a snipe cruiser ... Hec, just start feeding all the data in for these three traffic slots, then the western third of the formation, and we can ignore the rest of the archive for now, speed up the processing. I'll mark the boundaries for you here."

"Aye, Cap'n Caldy."

Twenty minutes later we nearly had our answer.

"Who's that?" Hector looked down at the display, where the suspect ships were now highlighted in their original deployment formation, time-stamped just after incursion reset.

Bart shook his head with uncertainty. "Some unit in 4th, that's the best I can do. I'd have to cross-reference with a standard formation diagram to get any more specific than that."

"Ah!" I lifted a finger. "I've got one, no doubt."

Hector looked at me with nervous skepticism.

"I assure you, Hector, my Cert authority quite includes incidental photography of the bridge. I'm sure I caught a deployment map at one point or another."

"'Kay, but ..."

I finished firmly, "And now that you and the AAS are paid data vendors, my authority and legal protections extend to your participation in this matter, as well."

At that the starhunter seemed placated. "Alright then."

I figured as much. My prior hand wringing on that fateful industrial street about whether the astronomers would want to be paid (and how) had been unnecessary. As it turned out, all AAS chapters relied on data bartering and sales to meet expenses and generally lubricate the field of astronomy, so the Third Street AAS already had several convenient data packages on offer, with standardized transaction agreements ready to sign.

The Society offered bargain rates, far below typical corporate consulting fees. (As one might expect; if there were much profit to be had the corporations would already have it themselves, after all.) For an all-inclusive whole-Vector package of the dates in question, with full raw-data archive, I parted with only #170,588.09, as my accountant will be glad to hear.

As I quickly sifted through my visual data from the CCIC at a nearby workstation, Hector remained hovering over Bart, and pointed down at the desk display. "Hold up."

"Mm?"

"In't that the sniffer? The little guy?"

"Maybe. Okay, yeah, I think so. What about it?"

"Why's he still movin'? Rest've been parked for a while, but he's not even in formation yet."

"Who knows, dawdling or something—anyway, look it's already slowing down at this time stamp to take position."

"Jupiter above, Caldy, we're still watchin' in reverse. Numpty. Wouldn't figure *you* havin' trouble identifyin' ass from face, even with sloppy trace like this," Hector snorted.

     TINY PLANET FILLED WITH LIARS

I looked up in time to catch Bart's embarrassed grimace. I probably should've scheduled the meeting for earlier in the day, he was clearly a bit tired. Then again, the appointment hadn't been made with him in mind (it took him several more weeks to trust Mira's team with my security—not that whipping out a bit of frantic scrying would've been any use in an emergency).

He muttered, "Oh … you're right. In fact … it's coming *into* the unit —fast. And still gaining velocity."

"Not into, *through*, friend. Lookit—run it back from 60 seconds earlier, in *forward* playback."

Having found what we needed in my personal files, I returned to the huddle in time to watch a small highlighted vessel approach the suspect sub-unit from the north—already at full burn—and blow right through the formation before continuing south toward the orbital skip's traffic slot in the rear. Several seconds later, the ships in the sub-unit began turning to follow the corvette down.

Bartimus looked up at me, eyes wide.

"Okay," I said carefully.

Hector looked back and forth between the two of us—I suspect he was enjoying the drama a bit. I handed him the file transfer to upload into the desk.

I said, "So. Let's see if there's a reasonable explanation to this or not. Matching please, Bart."

Bart nodded and began correlating my incidental footage of a formation diagram on a CCIC display with the Society's sensor data. A few minutes later he announced, "4th Division, Beta Battalion, Forward Screen Left, B Flight, Light Range Sub-Unit 19." He looked up, "For the main ships, anyway."

I nodded. Nothing notable about that sub-unit, as far as I knew, except that it was in 4th at all. "Now that," I said while pointing at the sprinting corvette.

Bartimus traced the ship back to its starting position. My throat tightened when he said quietly, "4th Division, Alpha Battalion, Forward Screen, A Flight, Recon Sub-Unit 1, Scout Squadron 1, Spotter 1."

"Okay," Hector said expectantly. "So ... the fuck does that mean?"

My breath went shallow, mind racing. I said distractedly, "Well, Bart? I'm sure it must've been in *all* the coterie newsletters at the time."

Bartimus' head snapped up and I instantly regretted my words, particularly mis-targeted as they were.

"I'm very sorry," I said immediately.

Bart shook his head, face reddening. "It's okay."

I swallowed and answered Hector. "4th Division's entire Forward Screen scouting operation engaged what is now a #530 billion contract three years ago for exclusive research and development of their latest signal suites, bidding war won by Vanderbilt Ascendant, Incorporated; whose CEO most likely tried to have me murdered just a few blocks from here in order to stop me from investigating this incursion. Bart, match the time stamp when that spotter violated lockdown with the launch of the orbital skip from Command Prime."

Bartimus nodded, and looked up a moment later. "It dropped out of position and went full burn 13 seconds after the skip launched."

Hector interjected, "Can't ya Cert up some fleet records and let the military explain their own damn selfs? What's that thick-ass paper o' yours for, anyway? *Just* impressin' plebs like us?"

I turned to him frankly. "There won't be any fleet records. The data was found to be corrupted immediately, for the entire incursion—before I'd even returned planetside, as it turns out. There won't be any accom-

 Tiny Planet Filled With Liars

panying announcement. In fact, outside the protection of my authority any civilian conversation about the topic is an imprisonable offense."

Hector whistled, then chuckled awkwardly. "This the same Cert s'pposed to be protectin' me and mine?"

"Yes." I looked him firmly in the eye.

He cocked his head and considered me for a few moments, closed mouth moving in contemplation. Finally he nodded. "Right, you'll be wantin' some dinner then, probably. Hope sandwiches are okay. That workstation next to you is mobile, you can move it closer if ya'need. Yell at anybody around if you need anything else for whatever ya'gotta do."

"Thanks, Hec," Bartimus called after as the astronomer set off. He reached out and squeezed my hand.

"Alright then," I said.

He turned back to the desk. "Let's see what else is hiding in these stars."

22

Admiral Seersa Kudaibergen

2nd Division "Bulwark" HQ, Floor 104, Conference Room 104.1

[Seersa Kudaibergen]

My understanding was—

[Interviewer]

With respect, Admiral—and I do say so with utmost sincerity, I'm sure you realize that—my duty to record a recalcitrant subject and avoid all ambiguity in such a case exceeds my desire to avoid offending you by making this a more formalized conversation.

...

I'm sure you understand.

[Seersa Kudaibergen]

Continue.

[Interviewer]

I—

...

Actually, pardon me, I feel we should—

...

Okay. I apologize for the reiteration.

[S.K.]

Of course.

[Int.]

Um, to reiterate, I have asked you for Command Prime's internal sensor records and all tactical data during the engagement in question, including in the hours directly following the battle, encompassing the SAR—excuse me—encompassing the search and recovery efforts, as well. Your response ...

[S.K.]

Unavailable due to technical error. You have my apologies.

[Int.]

The entire fleet.

[S.K.]

Mm.

[Int.]

Unfortunate.

[S.K.]

Indeed.

[Int.]

Alright. So, instead, I ask you again to review this astronomical data, which clearly seems to show—

[S.K.]

I'm afraid I object to your use of the word "clearly."

[Int.]

...

Mm-hmm.

...

Okay. Which myself *and* my legal associates believe comprises a record of insubordinate action on the part of multiple combat units in the fleet, directly following your own declaration of complete lockdown, excluding search and recovery activity.

…

As you can see here, a ranking spotter corvette and a significant portion of 4th Beta Battalion's Light Range Sub-Unit 19 are hundreds of kilometers out of position, in a return traffic slot that doesn't even lead to their—

[S.K.]

Excuse me, I'm sorry. I cannot recognize your identification of those ships. You have displayed no technical data confirming their identity—indeed no verified data of any kind, save your own supposition based on non-Corps civilian research archives of unknown origin or fidelity. *I* am not in a position to respond to supposition in deployment matters relating to combat. I have no idea who those units are or if they even genuinely exist, absent such legally sound verification.

[Int.]

(sharp exhalation) Then pretend.

…

I apologize. That is—let us assume for a moment that my team's analysis is correct. In the understanding that we are discussing a plausibly hypothetical scenario that may or may *not* have any bearing on the reality of the incursion engagement.

…

Okay?

[S.K.]

Mm.

[Int.]

Okay. Now. *If* these ships were indeed a forward screen sub-unit and front line spotter, would they not be out of position at this location, at the given time stamp?

[S.K.]

They would.

[Int.]

Would any of those vessels have any role whatsoever in search and recovery operations, which might justify their being out of position?

[S.K.]

They would not.

[Int.]

Are any of these three orbital return traffic slots anywhere near the slot those units *should* be taking back to their berthing installations, were my identification accurate?

[S.K.]

They are not.

[Int.]

And is *this* not the orbital skip launched directly from *your own* command ship, following Rear Admiral Smythe's local broadcast announcement that I—

[S.K.]

Excuse me—

[Int.]

Right, right, I'm sorry. *If* this were the skip launched directly from your own command ship—

...

 TINY PLANET FILLED WITH LIARS

Well.

(laughs)

I mean, Jupiter above. Would you be able to conceive of *any* justifiable reason for those ships to be there, given your own orders and the lockdown status of the entire fleet at the time?

[S.K.]

I would not.

[Int.]

Admiral ...

[S.K.]

Yes.

[Int.]

I—

...

Ah. That is—

...

Did you use me as bait?

(chuckles)

...

...

...

[recording pause]

23

Hector Luis Deshpande,
Bartimus Caldwell

*Third Street Amateur Astronomical Society,
Industrial District 12, Observatorium*

I GLANCED around, hoping to spy an uneaten sandwich on a plate somewhere, but came up short. I rubbed my face. "Bart, I don't know how I'm supposed to draw any conclusions about why the incursion nearly failed here. Even with the overlay I can't see anything worth seeing."

He sighed. "Yeah, I know ... neither can I. But I don't know what else we can do, the trace just isn't going to get any clearer when we've still got all of Fleet in the picture at these time stamps. The signals are too dense, I can't differentiate any further than this. If I let the degradation filter get any looser we'll practically be tagging vacuum itself."

I looked over at Hector. "And you?"

The astronomer shrugged. "If Caldy can't see any clearer in't no reason I'd be able to, he's got better feel than me to start with. Better'n anybody in the buildin' really, 'specially now he's all military drilled up and shit. All I see there is a whole lotta boom, boom, boom."

I nodded. Empirical data on scrying is uniformly antique and inconclusive, given how inscrutable the ability is, and how much variability exists in its manifestations between individuals. To wit, even beyond the "strength" of his skill itself, Bartimus was the only scry I'd ever met personally who seemed to rely so heavily on tactile sensation in the course of his workings, where Hector was in a more common statistical grouping and simply used his direct vision to examine and analyze sensor data —a method that's speculated to function as a biomnemonic technique shaping proprioception, or perhaps as an actual extension of same into the ocular fields. However, the starhunter would later describe it to me, simply, as "stalkin' the see-through shapes in the fog," which my research indicates is a generally representative self-account of his particular ability grouping. I'd once even met a scry whose skills were primarily aural in presentation, and I often lament not having taken notes of their description of listening to Jupiter.

Nonetheless, it was becoming clear that neither scryer was going to be able to generate a more conclusive finding from the engagement data, leaving me to make a case with a handful of wobbly, poorly defined sensor overlay "blobs" in the operational area of 4th Division's front line and forward left screen.

"Can we at least determine what *size* of unit is represented inside that blob? Is it a sub-unit? A whole battalion? What?"

Bartimus closed his eyes again, hands flitting over the desk display. He opened them and shook his head. "No. Definitely not a battalion, though. *Maybe* a flight. But I can definitely feel ... mmm ... I suppose I'd call it a reduction in armaments activity in the same area. Um—Hec, scrub this section here, over ... say ... five units in the time scale."

I watched as Hector played a 30-second chunk of the battle record back and forth while Bartimus' hands drifted slowly around his desk. After several minutes, he looked up and nodded with satisfaction. "Somewhere in this section an inconclusive number of ships are failing to participate in ... I'd say ... 30-to-40 percent of volley intervals."

My eyebrows shot up. "A *40 percent* reduction in local firepower?"

    Tiny Planet Filled With Liars

Bart squinted. "Just about ... on average, maybe more like 25 percent down net force in the highlighted region. It's hard to tell right off, since the astronomy equipment isn't specifically keyed to weapons signatures. But it's definitely all Alpha Corps signatures that are dropping in and out—Fleet armaments activity in this whole quadrant is stable and as I'd expect throughout. Maybe even a little heavier than usual, if I'm honest. I'd have to compare side-by-side with other recent engagements to know for sure. It feels a bit hotter than it should be, though ... I think. That's the best I can do."

I looked at the floor, shaking my head. "Why ... what objective would someone have to *not* fight? What possible reason ..."

Bartimus carefully cleared his throat. I looked up.

"I, uh ... I mean, it's nothing really, but I did happen to read a report last year about how salvage activity has plateaued in the last 15 years, and may even be declining based on occlusion detritus analyses from Beta Vector's half of the cycle."

I shrugged. "Okay." What would it matter? 'Salvage' was a euphemism for orbital debris clean-up, from everything I knew. Most of the recovered materials from destroyed Fleet Eternal vessels aren't even identifiable, much less usable; and even in those rare cases when our technology is capable of utilizing any such material, it's only because we can break it down into identifiable elemental molecules for our own manufacturing purposes. And there's certainly no shortage of elemental molecules in this system. And what would *not* fighting have to do with increasing Fleet salvage anyway? It made no sense.

But ...

I put an edge into my voice. "Bart?"

He shook his head. "Never mind, it doesn't mean anything. I don't know why I said it. The report's only conclusion was that we might be able to budget less for orbital maintenance in a few years."

I peered at him intently.

"Sandwiches?" Hector interjected.

"Oh yes, please," I instantly replied, Bart forgotten. "Especially if you've got more dosa shells back there."

"Come pick ya'self," Hector waved. I followed him immediately, stomach grumbling.

"Last I looked was 2600, what time is it now?" I wondered.

"Tomorrow," Hector laughed.

/|\

Bart rubbed his eyes.

I stood and stretched. "Alright, let's call it."

Hector jerked up from the desk he'd been falling asleep on, and said blearily, "Yeah?"

"Yeah. Bart and I are going to need several more days to complete the analysis of the entire formation, anyway. We'll handle it in my penthouse. I have enough to start with for my first interview with the admiral tonight—I'll start by focusing on the ... sniffer ship question for now."

Hector nodded and hauled himself upright. "Makes sense. Lemme ... uh ... Vem ... must be here to start her morning by now, we'll get the archives packed up for ya." He yawned and shuffled off.

I squeezed Bart's shoulder and we set about cleaning up the workstations we'd used. By the time Hector returned, we were prepared to leave.

The starhunter handed me a neatly tied parcel. "Fucker's riskin' the entire world here, in't he?"

I nodded.

"Mmm ... Fleet don't care what he wants. Fleet'll fuck us just the same."

I nodded.

"How long you think he been doin' this?"

"I don't know. Months, maybe. Perhaps a year or more, though that seems unlikely. Even without knowing what the purpose of this scheme is yet."

Hector nodded. "Okay. We keep minimum 20-year storage of archives. I'll send you the last 12 months, we'll get started on the data packages right away. No charge."

It was probably only the late (early) hour, but my chest tightened at the astronomers' generosity. I shook my head. "Thank you, friend. But I believe I'm actually going to need to put you and the Society on permanent retainer until further notice. Twenty million per year, to start. My publisher's lawyers will send the preliminary paperwork, make sure it's signed by all participating Third Street AAS officers with legal rights. The final contract signing will require stamped certification."

Hector's eyes widened. "Shit ... seriously?"

I murmured affirmatively.

"Uh, okay. Um ... you want ... I mean, we can re-tune our equipment for incursion days, if ya need. Closer to weapons signatures."

I held up a hand immediately. "No, please, and thank you. Let's not risk any ... undue attention. I am simply contracting with civilian astronomers for unused local overflow data and analysis. But I do need you to upgrade your security—and figure out how to segregate any among your number who *don't* wish to be exposed to this data, since its classification levels are raised by the very fact of my usage. I'm afraid for the duration of our relationship you'll need to bar such individuals from any area where you're dealing with archives authorized by my Cert, okay?"

Hector gestured, unconcerned. "No sweat. Everybody's gonna want on board, anyway, ya kiddin'?"

I chuckled. "I thought that might be the case. Oh—and, obviously, all such business is to be kept strictly confidential, even from other chapters in the Federation. I remain the only individual empowered to release or distribute data authorized by these Certs. As long as they don't know why you're requesting extraneous orbital records from other installations, there'll be no issues. But once that information is in your hands, as my duly authorized agents it is inherently classified. The lawyers will include an information security manual with the paperwork. Also, my accountant will be in touch with cost invoicing procedures. Send *all* expenses, but keep receipts for everything, she's a goddamn asshole otherwise."

"Hot data, hot credit. Gotcha."

While Bart began gathering our things, I called deeper into the observatorium, "Thank you, Vemda!"

Her voice drifted back, "That's Superior Logistics Warden Vemda, to you! You're welcome!"

Hector grinned. "She's workin' on buildin' up a partnership with some scries in a Gamma Vector settlement. Loves usin' her full title lately, pisses them off like crazy. You know how they hate pompery out there."

I laughed. Indeed.

"Oh! One more thing." The President Exemplar patted his pockets and pulled out a chit to place in my hand. He winked, "Plus one to the next orgy night."

I smirked but nodded graciously. "Thank you. And Bart?"

"Oh, he don't need no invite. *Bart*'s a permanent legacy."

Vemda's voice rang out, "YER FUCKIN' RIGHT HE IS!"

Bartimus bit his lip and tried to stifle a smile. I waved my eyes around with a sigh.

Horny consensual scientists. What're you gonna do.

24

Admiral Seersa Kudaibergen

*2ⁿᵈ Division "Bulwark" HQ, Floor 65,
Conference Room 65.1*

[Interviewer]

I understand.

...

But I must warn you—if you didn't enjoy the last interview, you're likely to enjoy today's topic even less.

[Seersa Kudaibergen]

Mm.

[Interviewer]

I'd like to present you with the—*unquestionably verifiable*—astronomical data I have analyzed from the period overlapping the incursion engagement itself.

[Seersa Kudaibergen]

I understand.

[Int.]

(chuckles)

...

...

Mmm. No, I believe we'll start here.

...

Okay.

[S.K.]

Yes.

[Int.]

This asset displays an analyzed region of the Alpha Corps formation five kilometers due east of the hinge point between the left front line and left flank screen. The highlighted region encompasses 60 percent of 4th Beta Battalion, 20 percent of 4th Alpha Battalion's Forward Screen A Flight, and an incidental mix of ships from other 1st and 4th Division units comprising less than five percent of force presence in the specified area.

[S.K.]

Are the boundaries of this area as arbitrary as they appear to be?

[Int.]

Yes and no.

[S.K.]

Mm.

...

I have no comment on your identification of those ships but acknowledge that those are the identities you will be referring to throughout your presentation.

[Int.]

Fine. Good enough to brew tea with.

[S.K.]

My grandmother used to say that all the time.

[Int.]

Likewise.

[S.K.]

Hm.

[Int.]

...

Admiral, I would like to confirm with you that it's your belief that some operational deficiency existed in or near your left flank deployments, necessitating your use of the emergency abort and Direct Drive orders issued during the engagement.

[S.K.]

...

...

...

I believe I can generally confirm the evident probability of that statement, by and large, absent a few details.

[Int.]

...

Okay.

...

I'm sorry, it's just—you know, it was only a single sentence, it only had "a few details" to start with.

(chuckles)

What's left, "absent" them?

[S.K.]

You'd be surprised.

[Int.]

…

Less than you might expect, I'm afraid.

…

Armaments analysis in this region clearly reveals that as much as 40 percent of the represented force strength is failing to participate in all indicated volley intervals. On average, the highlighted region exhibits 23 percent total down net force, from time of first contact to marker eight completion.

…

…

…

Admiral.

[S.K.]

Sincere apologies, was there a question?

[Int.]

Do you dispute anything I've said?

[S.K.]

Having neither analyzed the data myself nor read an authorized report of same from either AVOC or 2nd Division's own analysis units, I have no comment on your statement. I acknowledge your presentation.

…

Continue.

[Int.]

(sighs)

The, uh, the deficiency is discernible immediately. My analysts indicate a ten percent drop in firepower in this region of the formation in the first 15 seconds of the engagement, when compared to

   Tiny Planet Filled With Liars

an average of the last three incursions prior to February, which exhibit only a two percent variance in equivalent datasets. This percentage, as I've said, increases sharply over the course of last week's
incursion.

...

In a 20-second period spanning both your abort order and the Direct Drive override, TDNF hits a sustained peak of 38 percent. It
recovers to the neighborhood of 15 percent, until the last 15 seconds of the engagement, when it returns to 34 percent reduction
in force, sustained until stand down.

...

To put it directly, Admiral, our analysis indicates that each deficiency you felt obligated to counter with a corresponding Prime
order originated from the units in this specified region—though
sometimes as a rolling effect impacting combat performance elsewhere in the formation. My own analysts have examined the entirety of the Corps formation throughout the engagement. No
other units exhibit any detectably unusual behavior of any kind—
accounting for the aforementioned rolling effect, and the unusual
nature of the engagement itself, of course.

[S.K.]

...

Of course.

...

...

Continue.

[Int.]

You know, this isn't supposed to be a briefing.

[S.K.]

It is not.

[Int.]

...

Of course.

...

Despite your dispute of those calculations—ah. Pardon me. Wrong ... uh, note. Obviously, you (sighs) haven't disputed—apologies, one moment.

...

...

I prepared for a very ... uh ... specific sort of—flow chart, no, skip that—um ... contentiousness ... uh ...

[S.K.]

Take as much time as you need.

[Int.]

...

(clears throat)

...

TDNF in all other units in the formation is within the usual variance—in this case, somewhere in the neighborhood of two-point-five percent ...

[S.K.]

I see.

[Int.]

Admiral, I—I have to admit I think this calls for more ... I mean I would have thought more—for godsake, a Fleet Eternal vessel found its way through the front lines *inside* the indicated region and destroyed a *bulwark*! Leading directly to the loss of 23 ships and ... nineteen-thousand-four-hundred-eighty-five deaths! Nearly *forty-thousand* DIA casualties have occurred over the last two incursions, and if your orders hadn't incidentally moved the entire west quadrant behind the battle line there would certainly be *many* thousands more among that number now! The complete breakdown in attrition prevention protocols alone *demands* action, does it not?

[S.K.]

Mm.

[Int.]

Admiral! I was *on* that bridge! I can pull up my own footage of CCIC displays isolating the attack on that bulwark as we SPEAK and show you—

[S.K.]

Go on then.

[Int.]

—a single mammoth class laser boat in range! Right there! A *single* ship providing rear and point defense for an entire bulwark quarter!

[S.K.]

I see.

[Int.]

Five other vessels assigned to point defense on that bulwark which should *not* have retreated with the main line during the abort or DD maneuvers ... did so nonetheless. I can time stamp the precise instant they become individually detectable again following Fleet's withdrawal ... correlated here—where they are *quite* clearly in formation with the two units I discussed earlier, nearly 18 kilometers off their own posts, for no discernibly legitimate operational reason, leaving that bulwark to perform its secondary withdrawal needlessly vulnerable to assault! Which begs the question: What were they doing in the prior seconds that left them so out of position by the end?!

(audible breathing)

...

Admiral! I *demand* your response!

[S.K.]

Indeed.

...

I believe that will suffice.

[Int.]

What—

[S.K.]

You have the raw data archives to back this up, and will be including them in your filed report?

[Int.]

I—what? Y-yes. Yes, of course I do. Will. I will.

[S.K.]

Right. May I escort you to the foyer?

[Int.]

What? Admiral—

[S.K.]

Unless you'd like to accompany Jon and I while we take dinner in the flag dining room, that is. I do recommend the obsidian tea service, it's well worth the visit.

[Int.]

...

...

Yes, okay.

  TINY PLANET FILLED WITH LIARS

[S.K.]

You may turn that off now.

[Int.]

(sighs)

Yes, sir.

25

Sato Prelate Victrox Hampurdinck

Crystal City Temple of Jupiter, Floor 21, Clergy Parlor

[Interviewer]

No, thank you.

[Victrox Hampurdinck]

You're quite sure?

[Interviewer]

I've said no. Thank you.

[Victrox Hampurdinck]

...

Curious, it's my experience that most visitors are quite eager to partake of the snuffing ceremony. It's something of a tourist appeal. I assure—

[Int.]

Prelate, I have no intention of spending the rest of the day with the reek of fermented rosepowder lodged in my nasal cavities. Thank you.

[V.H.]

In proxy then, as I partake. To the Sky and Jupiter Abo—

[Int.]

No.

[V.H.]

...

Ah. Ah, I see.

...

Forgive me. As you might imagine, I tend to presume the faith of visitors to this temple. Even when—in any case, my apologies. Perhaps it's a habit I should reconsider.

[Int.]

Perhaps.

[V.H.]

Shall we sit, then?

[Int.]

Thank you.

[V.H.]

...

...

I presume no objection to ... yes? Unbottled yesterday from the upper larder, 40-year vintage. I recommend a few milliliters of water to top off—in that carafe—at your discretion, of course.

[Int.]

Fine. Just a half measure, thank you.

[V.H.]

Certainly.

...

Full measure, myself, I have no evening service today.

(chuckles)

   TINY PLANET FILLED WITH LIARS

...

...

Cool cube? No?

...

...

There we are.

[Int.]

Mm.

[V.H.]

I must say, I was rather surprised to receive your missive, particularly once it became clear that—

[Int.]

I am here to discuss Crowley Vanderbilt.

[V.H.]

...

(clears throat)

...

Yes. As I was saying, I was surprised once it became clear that you
intended to present questions related to a member of my own
temple, which, as you may have been unaware, is not permitted by
the doctrine of this particular sect.

[Int.]

Noted. I wield Cert authority, shall we begin?

[V.H.]

(clears throat)
Of course the tradition of treating such doctrines in parity with
classification codes is long-established, quite—

[Int.]

How long has Crowley Vanderbilt attended this temple?

[V.H.]

…

…

…

Are you familiar with the Crystal City district?

[Int.]

When was the first time Crowley Vanderbilt attended this temple?

[V.H.]

…

…

…

Mr. Vanderbilt's entire family has attended this temple exclusively for as long as I care to remember.

[Int.]

He was initiated into the Church of Jupiter in this temple?

[V.H.]

Once he came of age, of course. As I was saying, the Crystal City district is a fascinating slice of—

[Int.]

How much has Crowley Vanderbilt personally invested in the church, specifically this temple's portfolio, and when may I expect your coterie records of those transactions?

…

…

…

[recording pause]

/|\

[Int.]

That has not been my experience—and I *would* like to move on. I was only planning for a 20-minute meeting.

[V.H.]

How can you say such a thing? There are no less than three thousand sects on this world in any given year, am I to be accountable to the entire universe of Jovian beliefs? Every sect? Every temple throughout the entire Church?

[Int.]

No. Just yours.

[V.H.]

And am I—did you just turn that thing back on?

[Int.]

Yes.

[V.H.]

(chuckles)

Fine. And am I now to serve as your source, in utter violation of my faith, only because—

[Int.]

Your faith does not concern me, Prelate. The customs by which the church vacillates at whim between apolitical shielding and explicitly political action do not concern me. Whether your sect has been around for days or years does not concern me. My Cert is authorized by law. I will exercise it by force of same.

...

Now, if we could.

[V.H.]

...

...

...

You know, I must confess, I've never understood the non-faithful. I find it difficult to envision the interiority of a person who can live in a system like this and *not* smell the divine on the winds.

[Int.]

A system like this?

[V.H.]

Quite obviously, in my opinion. A bilateral system unlike any other? A single planet and its single moon locked in a shared orbit on *opposite* sides of their star? No other satellites of any more significance than asteroids, all the way to the outermost bounds of the star's sphere of influence?

[Int.]

Indeed.

[V.H.]

Unprecedented. Is it not? Does the *science* not say there is no analogue to this planetary system in the known universe? Nowhere else ... mmm ... such a specifically particular arrangement of heavenly bodies, balanced to an equilibrium beyond all known reasoning?

[Int.]

Are you making a claim that the system is inherently *proof* of divinity? Because—

[V.H.]

And why not, eh? Why not! Take Jupiter itself—what an absurdity! Less than half the size of the nearest effective equivalent star classification—twice as dense, twice as bright, a fraction of the usual magnitude variability—absurd! In more than 300 years of recorded astronomy and astral physics, no empirically sound theory has ever withstood the scrutiny of time as way of explanation for *that*. Has it? Eh?

...

...

...

Your own ignorance—ours—even after so many years of searching, and, and ... such consistency in findings among *all* other systems in known space ... that is the undoing of your particular stance on this question, I would say.

...

Refill?

[Int.]

(sighs)
Thank you.

...

...

...

You know what strikes me as absurd.

[V.H.]

(chuckles)
Go ahead.

[Int.]

How vigorously you will expound on the possibility of Jupiter's divinity, even while I know you'll react just as strongly against the very suggestion that Fleet is, in actuality—

[V.H.]

(laughs)

Ah, so you really do have an absurdity of your own to discuss.

[Int.]

Precisely.

...

You know, many would say that this is just a planet, a moon, and a star. In an unusual configuration, most certainly, but nonetheless. Just that. Perfectly within the realm of our current understanding, *and* perfectly understandable regarding our confusion in the meanwhile. We live within such a small pocket in this existence, after all ... we are utterly alone, trying to see our own face without aid of a mirror.

...

It's bound to take some time. Especially when we're trying to figure out what face we *used* to wear.

...

How couldn't it?

...

...

But Fleet, now. Fleet makes ... no sense. Fleet is, as yet ... *utterly* beyond fathom. Not a single indication as to its purpose, or why we are its target. No sign of active intelligence, no sign of life as we know it, no recorded communication or signal of *any* kind, in hundreds of years. Who would design such a force to begin with? Who? How ... with such overwhelming strength, yet so easily

     Tiny Planet Filled With Liars

routed into retreat? So easily distracted from attacking the planet's surface by even relatively token resistance in orbit? Returning month, after month, after month ... after month ... undissuaded ... un- ...

...

...

...

If you ask me, priest, *Fleet* is the only hint of divinity raising its head out there, if such a thing were to ever exist.

...

And it's certainly not out to reward us for faith.

[V.H.]

...

...

...

Interesting.

...

I disagree. As does the Church, or at least those parts I care about.

[Int.]

And the archaeopetro-layer? How is that supposed to fit into your framework? What divinity in the history of this system accounts for *that*?

[V.H.]

How is it supposed to fit into *yours*?

[Int.]

...

...

...

(chuckles) Alright. The petro-layer is a wholly agnostic mystery, I concede.

[V.H.]

Mm-hmm. Refill to that.

[Int.]

No, thank you.

[V.H.]

I don't mind.

...

...

[loud crystal clinking]

[V.H.]

Mmm.

...

...

...

You know, I do understand your antagonism.

[Int.]

...

Indeed?

[V.H.]

Please, do believe me. It feels as if you've—perhaps understand-ably—taken the wrong lesson from your ... professional experi-ence.

[Int.]

Professionally experiencing summary discharge due to simple biol-ogy, you mean? At least that was the miserable excuse flogged at the time.

[V.H.]

Please, understand, it's not ... Yes, I agree, that was an unfortunate
period of zeal among certain sects—

[Int.]

Zealotry.

[V.H.]

Mm?

[Int.]

Zealotry. Not zeal; zealotry.

[V.H.]

...

—among certain sects, and it's only a quirk of political fate that
such voices happened to gain prominence in a period ... suscepti-
ble to—

[Int.]

The punishment of innocents in service of obscuring fear and ha-
tred, and not incidentally agglomerating political power in certain
coterie spheres.

[V.H.]

Please understand. It's not *you* they took issue with, it's your *body*.
There's something wrong with your *body*.

[Int.]

(snorts)

...

Jupiter's light touches us all, priest.

...

Their grandchildren's grandchildren will look more like me than
like you. They will be *shaped* more like me than like you—to

whatever extent you can *divine* the difference even as you speak to a guest.

...

...

They know this. You know this. Every cell on this planet bathes in it, even now. Skin to spinal cord.

...

Tell me, would you even *know*, if you weren't already familiar with my personal history? I mean, know *specifically*? ... Would *most* people?

...

...

...

So don't insult me with further alibis on their behalf, godammit. *I* require none. I lived it.

...

Don't look to me to absolve you through their sins.

[V.H.]

...

I desire only to make clear how futile it can be to try and impose ideological uniformity onto a fundamentally ... diverse ... assemblage of ... beliefs.

[Int.]

...

Prelate.

[V.H.]

Yes?

[Int.]

I am investigating a failure in the defense of this world which I believe can be tied, at least in part, directly to Crowley Vanderbilt.

[V.H.]

...

...

...

Interesting.

[Int.]

Crowley Vanderbilt attempted to have me assassinated for this effort not three weeks ago.

[V.H.]

...

May I review the Constabulary report?

...

...

Oh. Oh I see.

[Int.]

(sighs)

...

Prelate, Vanderbilt has referenced this temple multiple times in
support of proof-of-character filings in various actions. In fact,
lesser priests have offered sworn testimony in such matters on no
less than three occasions, as you doubtless know.

[V.H.]

(sniffs)

[Int.]

The day after his attempt on my life he chose to stand in line at
this very temple for a blessing, during which time he conspicuously appeared on live broadcast, as demonstration of his faith
and stewardship.

...

...

...

Prelate, you lay claims to a distance between his activities and
those of this temple which are not supported by fact, of *any* ideological persuasion.

[V.H.]

I believe this meeting has come to its end. Thank you most sincerely for the company and diversion, on what would otherwise
certainly have been an idle afternoon.

[Int.]

Prelate—

...

...

(sighs)

...

The temple will receive a formalized reiteration of my request for
all financial records relating to Crowley Vanderbilt. Failure to
comply or present plans to do so will yield a notification of Cert
breach in faith, recorded and reported to the Central Office of
Applied Thought.

[V.H.]

(clears throat)
I understand.

[Int.]

Thank you for your time.

26

Jieun Marks,
Swain Lieutenant (ret.) Abigail Zukas
Marks/Zukas Residence, District 61

AS YOU may have already surmised, COAT received yet another breach in faith notification some days following my meeting with the Prelate, which it duly opted to disregard.

In fact, other than an imminent visit to AVDC's Detention Center IV, it would be quite some time before I ever again received the explicit cooperation of *any* official actor in the course of enforcing my Cert rights. At least when acting in their official capacities.

Glory to the Returns?

Accordingly, as mid-month approached, and my work with Bart and the March sensor analysis had come to its end, I was forced to begin filling my calendar with less bureaucratically-inclined subjects. Fortunately, one such pair of subjects found *me*, via a cryptic ad in a regional newspaper referencing a missing son, who served in 1st Division. Said ad begged for any information from any knowledgeable parties. Though it had run more than four weeks prior by the time I came across it while reviewing old articles, the posting couple were still quite eager to meet in person following my initial contact, in which I had only vaguely described my ongoing enterprise. I'm not sure why I reached out to them at all, in honesty; except that I felt an intense burst of kinship with somebody seeking answers so fervently as myself. I certainly hadn't recognized their son's name, and hadn't expected such to begin with. I would not burden them with Cert responsibilities, and approached it as a purely civilian engagement. A personal matter, explicable or otherwise.

However.

If you have never seen firsthand the light in the eyes of a parent who believes she's about to hear news from a lost child ... may you also never face the injury of having no such news on offer.

It is to Jieun's great credit that she nonetheless invited me in promptly, taking my jacket to shelve while she introduced me to her wife and retired Swain Lieutenant, Abigail Zukas.

Zukas appeared to be nearing her eighties, and still exhibited old traces of that much gruffer period in military history, even in her civilian repose. I admit I found her occasional anachronism quite charming, especially because she'd likely only retired a few years prior. The thought of her heavy steps plodding across ship catwalks while she growled orders at increasingly fripperous underlings over the decades ignited a nostalgia which I rarely feel otherwise.

Competence. Perhaps that's the word I missed so dearly. Rare at any age, seemingly.

In any case, Zukas mixed a pleasantly stiff Aurelian Sunset; strong enough to prevent my feeling guilty when it became clear that the two parents had decided their task was to comfort *me*, as my expressions of investigative frustration kept punctuating the initial discussion, despite my efforts to maintain both classifications and propriety. I'd begun to feel the days pass like drum beats, by then, and the toll was mounting.

But once we'd all settled into our second Sunset and the conversation had taken a more unwound turn, Zukas lifted her glass in examination, her thoughts starting to wander alongside the intermingling currents of the liqueurs.

  Tiny Planet Filled With Liars

She said, "You know, Caio apologized to me when he received his assignment."

I chuckled. "I can imagine."

She waved a hand dismissively, lips twitching upward despite herself. "Pointless. Stupid boy. As if I ever gave him reason to think I had any cares about the rivalry between 1st and 2nd his whole childhood. What a waste of time. But of course, these days ... anyway, he'd obviously been hearing about it constantly from the very first day of drill, wanted me to know he'd never ... *ever* let it come between us. Said he already told his bunk crew, 'I come from a *mixed Division household* so fight me or shut up.'"

She laughed, a surprisingly melodious sound considering her graveled speaking voice. "He was so young then. Stupid boy." Her eyes began to shine, and Jieun reached over to take her hand.

Jieun said, "He told us when his leave was over at the end of Stellary that he'd be back for a weekend early February, maybe end of January—for Abby's birthday. He shipped out, then only called home *once* in mid-January, then ..."

Zukas cleared her throat and reached up to straighten Jieun's collar, which had rolled up on itself. "Never even got a letter for the February incursion, or March ... he always sent at least a little note if he couldn't call—even when we were *both* up there, he'd still send a kiss or something to Ji back home. But that was the last we've heard."

I nodded. "Where exactly is he stationed in 1st?"

"UFD Balabalo, missile cruiser—we think deployed somewhere in one of the chop-n-block patches up north, at least it was back in February. Who knows since then." Zukas took a long drink before concluding, "But of course they don't tell you shit when you're just a parent."

Forward screen, then. Yes. I nodded. Nod. Nod.

She sighed. "You know, when I first signed on ... was just after 1ˢᵗ had its tantrum and renounced the Admiralty, had that big ridiculous abdication ceremony once they knew the bulwarks were definitely sticking around and the old battle plans were really dead. No more mobile ranks. Their precious battleships not the biggest dicks on the line anymore ..."

She took another drink, head shaking. "They'd have accepted any attrition rate in the world, long as they could keep their chins in the air, wouldn't they? Didn't give even one tiny shit about how much better the bulwarks are at minimizing brain melts on the front. Irrelevant to them. They'd *still* rather be out there parading naked ships back and forth across the line, strutting high turnover product, dodging scuttled corpses ... Thank Jupiter we changed ways."

She tapped her glass, tracing fingers through the condensation on its surface. "I remember how we were all supposed to be *so fucking excited* that 2ⁿᵈ would *always* be in Prime Command from then on, no more switching back and forth with 1ˢᵗ every other year." She snorted. "Those first five years I was on one of the teams that always had to be reporting our deployment tonnage directly to AVOC after every incursion, so 1ˢᵗ could make sure they had just a *little bit* more weight deployed the next month, to stay ahead of us without having to spend too much more. That's around the time they switched the Division ident to 'Hammer,' quiet down the ones on the Board bawling to quadruple ship manufacturing and swamp 2ⁿᵈ out of the sky. Jupiter above. 'Hammer' and 'Bulwark.'" She shook her head. "Idiots. Both sides. As if we didn't have more important things to worry about up there."

I "mmm"ed in agreement.

She rested her hand on her stomach. Her voice thickened. "I know he's just under shut-the-fuck-ups. Some ... operation, maybe. Or classified training. I know the Corps ... just sometimes likes to fuck around with deployments, even once you've been brushing rank for a while. I

  TINY PLANET FILLED WITH LIARS

know." Her hand had begun to knead the flesh beneath. "But when someone's lived *inside you*, 'knowing' isn't enough ... I need to *Know*. You know." She reached up and wiped her face. "I think I deserve at least that much from them, after all these years."

She carefully lifted the glass to her lips, eyes relaxing into thought again.

Jieun said quietly, "Was a rough incubation span, with Caio. I'd ... we'd already lost one the year before. A daughter. We were barely getting by on her Corps salary at the time, I'd been cut from my job at the organix printer before I'd even got pregnant, then got sick in month seven ... Tried to get me into a hospital early, but even with Abby's 2nd privileges, nowhere we could afford had a room available in time, except a no-fee incu-clinic ... she ..."

Jieun rubbed her mouth and leaned into Zukas. "Anyway. When *she* started to carry the next year, we prayed so hard ... made *triple* hospital reservations, one for each of the last three months. I stopped eating for a week here and there, to help us save up, and make sure she and the bundle always had plenty. She didn't know. Probably would've killed me if she had, I was still supposed to be on recuperation."

Zukas snorted affirmatively.

Jieun continued, "We spent her whole pregnancy holding our breaths. Especially since Abby's a little older'n me, right? And life was still hard. Harder than now, anyway. And we'd waited a little longer than maybe we should've to start with, knowing we'd definitely wanted a child ... two, actually, back then ... you know how time slips off. Of course she did great by the end, eventually even got a half refund on our first two reservations, but we didn't know that yet ... Even once it passed viability and became *he*. How could we ever feel safe, even then? Hmm? Not after the year before. Not yet. Not without ... without seeing *him*, right? Like, he's not part of this world until he's *really* part of it, right?

How do we know for sure it's not just a part of ourselves we're feeling again? A trick inside ourselves, again ... about to disappear ... Until we can really *see* him. See his little body moving. Touch him with real hands. Smell him. Hear him. Really—"

Her breath shuddered and her shoulders began to shake.

Zukas put her drink down and passed her wife a silk. She smiled gently at me and laid a hand on Jieun's leg. "We're just starting to worry that he's not really part of this world anymore. Really worry. I'm sure you understand."

I nodded, mute with shame.

Because I did understand by then. Had understood as soon as she'd said the ship's name, even as it had been joined by dozens more in the weeks since.

I'm sorry, Abby.

27

Lieutenant (Junior Grade) Naomlo Kekoa

Alpha Vector Defense Corps Detention Ct. IV, Level(s) 181/195, Legal Anteroom(s)

[Interviewer]

—or so they've said.

[Naomlo Kekoa]

Who gives a single scintillating shit? I mean, really? The fuck else do I have on the schedule today?

...

HEAR THAT BEN? I KNOW YOU CAN HEAR ME FUCKER! GO 'HEAD, COME ON IN AND CUT US SHORT, I'LL BITE YOUR DICK RIGHT THE FUCK OFF. SHOVE YOUR TIME LIMITS UP YOUR ASS!

...

...

Fucker took drill with me, bunked in camp the first couple months even. We fuckin' *cried* together after a piss-to-shit night run in those fuckin' boots tore our feet up one time. Now I'm just the prisoner and he gets a paid vacation planetside to join the security detail and 'represent ship command.'

(snorts)

...

Least these cell slippers are COZY AS FUCK.

[Interviewer]

Lieutenant, if we could. I agree the PTS marathon bond should be sacred, your claim to shameful betrayal is valid, and so forth—but as I've said, my allotted time here is limited.

[Naomlo Kekoa]

You got all that? Include it in the report.

[Int.]

Yes, I am also recording.

...

"bite your dick right ... the fuck off," yes, word-for-word.

[N.K.]

(laughs)
Fuckin' right.

[Int.]

Don't misunderstand me, I have no question about why you feel the way you do. With regards to being here at *all,* your anger is certainly wholly justified.

[N.K.]

Holy justified. I like that.

[Int.]

...

Uh, yes. To begin, I'd—

[sound of opening door]

[Int.]

Ex*cuse* me—

[out of capture voice]

     TINY PLANET FILLED WITH LIARS

[Int.]

What? Then why would you even bring us to *this* room to begin with?

[out of capture voice]

[Int.]

For Jupiter—alright ... But take a message to your superiors directly afterward: Disrupting this interview again leads *right* back here, only they won't be on that side of the door once I'm through with them.

...

You understand me?

...

Then yes, go ahead.

[N.K.]

And send Ben in after us when we get there, you piece of shit. I SEE YOU BACK THERE FUCKER!

...

[recording pause]

/|\

[Int.]

Okay.

[N.K.]

You think they'll try again?

[Int.]

Uh ... doubtful. How much smaller can a room—ah, could you move your elbow, please, my recorder—

[N.K.]

Sorry.

[Int.]

No, it's quite—oops, apologies, that's my knee. Let me—

[audible scraping]

[N.K.]

No I'll twist this way.

[Int.]

...

...

There we are.

(sighs)

[N.K.]

Naw, you're right, I don't think there's any smaller rooms they can try next. Look, you can see the mop brackets on the wall there, right behind you where the window is glued in.

...

Hey, how'd they even get the table in here? Did it fuckin' *sprout* here?

[Int.]

...

(sighs)

[N.K.]

Could you really have 'em lock-n-keyed, if they fuck with us again?

[Int.]

I can certainly try.

[N.K.]

(chuckles)

Mm.

…

…

(chuckles) Mmm.

…

Okay. Go ahead.

[Int.]

…

One moment.

…

…

…

Right.

…

Okay. You are Lieutenant Junior Grade Naomlo Kekoa.

[N.K.]

Yes, sir.

[Int.]

Please don't call me that, I am not a service member.

[N.K.]

Oh yeah? Well shit, even better. For a second there thought you was just high up enough to not hafta uniform. Fuck those fuckin' fuckers, right? Pompous pricks.

[Int.]

(chuckles)

Right.

…

If you could, please state the charges under which you are de-
tained.

[N.K.]

(groans)

(clears throat)

"Lieutenant, you are hereby remanded to custody and relieved of
all positional 4th Division privileges for a period of no less than
one month pre-trial, on the charges of willful mis-use and destruction of Alpha Vector Defense Corps property and failure to obey
orders not received."

...

YOU HEAR THAT FUCKERS? NOT RECEIVED! YOU'D
ALL BE FUCKIN' ASHES IF NOT FOR ME, PIECE OF SHIT!
THEY'RE MAD 'CAUSE I DIDN'T LET YOU *BURN!* YOU
HEAR THAT BEN? BEN!

[Int.]

Lieutenant.

[N.K.]

Sorry.

...

Sorry.

[Int.]

Quite alright.

...

Ah, whoops, skipped—uh. Please state your name, rank, assignment, and position—uh, at the time of the March incursion, obviously.

[N.K.]

Naomlo Kekoa, Lieutenant Junior Grade, 4th Beta Forward Screen Left, UFD Martial Horizons 3, second-line Defensive Officer.

[Int.]

Had you been assigned to that laser boat for long?

[N.K.]

About a year, I think. Maybe more, by now, shit.

[Int.]

Mm-hmm. With the same position throughout?

[N.K.]

Yeah. Been through three first-line DOs meantime, but I was always second.

[Int.]

Indeed? Seems like an unusually high turnover rate for such a key position.

[N.K.]

Is it? Seems pretty standard, long as I've been enlisted.

[Int.]

Hm.

...

...

And your duties?

[N.K.]

Command dissemination and logistics, mostly.

[Int.]

As compared to the first-line ...

[N.K.]

Same, they just get to speak first and yell more.

[Int.]

(laughs)

Yes, that sounds about right.

[N.K.]

I did most of the admin bullshit around there the last six months anyway. Once they made me go through the *second* month-long "temp" period of suddenly havin' it rammed into my own duty schedule while the first-line DO was switched out and orientated again, I just forgot to tell the last one that it was his responsibility, kept doin' it myself instead. Less hassle.

(laughs)

Oh shit, that means they got a first-line DO now who in't got no fucking clue how to handle the rebuild paperwork, don't it.

(laughs)

...

...

(laughs)

[Int.]

I see.

...

Lieutenant, if you could, please explain to me the general operational parameters of the boat's field hardening systems.

[N.K.]

(still chuckling)
What, like ... ?

[Int.]

How it should function, how it should *not* function, what guide-lines you adhere to in the course of field operation, and so on.

[N.K.]

Ah, okay, so, basically, the field is just a multi-phase dynaelectro-magnetic system that runs like a river, right? Most of the time overwash from the PD reactors is enough to keep the generator buzzing, at least on a laser boat like that. FHG pumps the river out, it's routed through the ship to be embedded inside every outer armor surface on the hull. All the charge differential goes in one direction, automatically configured to whatever the "rear" is at the time, and if somethin' goes smack into the field, it sucks up most the energy from the impact, redirects and slips it off, then spews it out the back end into space.

...

It's dispersal more than hardening, point'a fact, but nobody gives a shit if a name makes any fuckin' sense around here. If I had my fuckin' say—should be Field Dispersal Generator, really. Or ... or maybe Dispersal Field Gen—

[Int.]

Mm-hmm. How is this field normally used during incursions—*typical* incursions, that is?

[N.K.]

Barely at all, bein' honest, though I know the fuckers're gonna try and twist that fact to do me in.

...

I mean, FHG's on. It's always on during active combat, of course. Even if we didn't need it for defense, it's still soaking up overflow from the laser emplacements, we'd have to find somethin' else to do with those power eddies otherwise. But it's really only sup-posed to be there to help the armor slip away as much spillover ra-diation as it can, coming off the bulwarks. We're not supposed to be taking more than incidental hits ourselves. The fuck's the bul-wark *for* then, right? I mean, damn.

...

Not supposed to.

[Int.]

I see. And this time?

[N.K.]

Well, this time I used it to save the fuckin' ship, in't it?

[Int.]

Agreed ... but.

[N.K]

(groans)
Alright, so, you're me, right? Lookin' at the board—no, fuckit, I wasn't looking at the board then, I didn't fucking *have to*, I could see that fucking thing coming right at us on the opticals.

[Int.]

I can imagine.

[N.K.]

So, you're me, right? See that fucker coming our way, spiraling ev-erywhere, outta control ... Cap' got the boat spinning that mam-moth ass around its own damn self, near ready to vom' just watchin' the optical processors try to keep up with the speed ... but I just knew, somehow. Knew we were gonna take it. Right on the lips.

...

 Tiny Planet Filled With Liars

So, you know your FHG is your only hope, and that it in't got half the eggs it needs to get the job done, right? But it maybe *can*—just not with SOP.

...

So ... (chuckles) so you just dump the whole ship straight through those fuckin' circuits at the last second, right after we took some kinda big hit on the ass. Just before that Fleet fucker plowed our neck. Every fuckin' bit, down to the last fucker fuckin' millijoule. Down the river. Right down the fuckin' pipes.

...

(whispers) *Fuck.*

[Int.]

The primary power grid?

[N.K.]

Mm-*hmm*! Lucky that hit to the cheeks knocked everything aft of Engineering Control offline, freed up shit loads of power, all piled up waitin' for nowhere to go. Near burned my hand clean the fuck off—lookit this fucker, you don't wanna know what's under this bandage, but you can see it in't fuckin' much.

[Int.]

I'm sorry.

[N.K.]

Don't be, I'm still here bitchin' about it, so I don't GIVE A SHIT WHAT THOSE PIECES OF SHIT SAY.

...

I did what I could with what I had, and now I live. Now *all* those fuckers live.

...

FUCK YOU BEN.

[Int.]

Forgive me, Lieutenant. Obviously I'm not an engineer, but it's my understanding that what you're describing shouldn't be possible. Do you even have access to the PPG controls in the Defensive Operations suite?

[N.K.]

Well, no. Not as such, know what I mean.

[Int.]

I'm afraid I don't.

[N.K.]

...

...

...

(chuckles)

Fuckit. Engineering pod had been in there working the grid off and on all month long. I'm gettin' poked by one of them, she's comfortable with me, she started stashing her gear in my desk, instead of havin' to haul it around three times a week. Logical, you know. In't harming no one.

...

So I slapped every FHG shunt relay I could get my hands on, near ripped the limiter offset switch out the board, yanked her engineering control box offa my desk, smacked it into the nearest unlocked PPG panel and dumped the fuckers like a big fuckin' hero.

...

BIG FUCKIN' HERO.

...

It's not like I planned it. Had what, ten, twenty seconds? I didn't think, I just knew I had this, and this, and this, and so I did *that*.

   Tiny Planet Filled With Liars

...

Fuck.

[Int.]

Quite a fortunate set of circumstances, especially considering the bulwark's ablation reactor lost containment several seconds after your collision with the Fleet vessel. I'm sure you know by now— even being in here and with it being classified—but none of the other ships within a kilometer of that blast survived intact.

[N.K.]

Yeah TELL THAT TO THESE GREASELICKIN' **PIECES OF SHIT!** BEN.

[Int.]

(chuckles) Jupiter above.

...

Noted.

[N.K.]

Sorry. Lot echoey in here than you'd think, huh?

[Int.]

Quite.

[N.K.]

(whispers) Fuck you, Ben.

28

The Interviewer, Bartimus Caldwell
Pleiades Tower, Penthouse Supreme

DESPITE MY best efforts to further cultivate productive sources, I approached the end of March with nothing actionable to show for it save boiling frustration and a mounting certainty that I'd lost any opportunity to prevent Vanderbilt's plan from progressing. By then I would have settled for any firm details about what the scheme was to begin with, particularly since I'd recently received confirmation that 2nd Division could not accommodate my request to observe the imminent April incursion. As far as I could foresee at the time, that marked the end of my last reasonable opportunity to gain any new intelligence firsthand. My sterile rage at the (not unexpected) news was only slightly ameliorated by the hot flush of relief that I wouldn't need to endure further combat in person. But the urge to find an answer—any answer—was still paramount.

In such attempt, I convened with Bart the evening after the scouting engagement of end March to see if any new insights could be drawn from the attendant astronomical data, which had arrived via security courier from the AAS that afternoon (signed: "Love, Hector & V – Mo-MoMo [kissy face drawing]").

I'd had Bart select and order a new scrying desk and data workstation to be installed in the penthouse, which had arrived a few days prior (and, annoyingly, required several additional power conduits routed to

the suite). After an hour of fruitlessly trying to pry him away from coo-
ing over his new sensorial throne, I finally abandoned the dining room
and had the server arrange our dinner on a table in the office instead.
Here Bart could blindly reach behind for a bite without having to spare
a second from the top-of-the-line, high-contrast, max-projection augmented holographic arrays featured in his chosen model, the Xatarax Ultimate Mk3 (#125 million, custom).

Fortunately his technological ardor remained unquenched when I
finished my own meal and silently swapped whatever sample array he'd
been playing with for the Society's latest scouting data. But some minutes afterward, he suddenly froze in place with a quiet cry of surprise.

I looked up from the workstation, where I'd been reading Vemda's
memorandum (attached to the archive) outlining her suggestion to
bring a non-Federation Gamma Vector scrying installation into our little
Cert circle, in pursuit of expanding the scope of our working data fields.
Though I was not particularly enthused by the thought of making classifications maintenance even more complex—never mind with a *franchise*
—I could see the utility in having a trace source located so distantly from
Alpha Vector, what with its mess of Fleet energy signatures muddying
every incursion.

But with my attention now broken, I reached out and nudged Bart
expectantly. "What?"

Instead of answering, he began moving his arms through the holographic data clouds surrounding him, eyes closed, lips fluttering in a
constant muttered stream. I sighed and attempted to return to my reading, knowing there was no point in wielding further impatience now.

For nearly ten minutes Bart pored over the data, first centimeter-by-
centimeter in a methodical survey, then with mounting frenzy; a darting
arm here, a finger curling urgently there.

 Tiny Planet Filled With Liars

Finally he looked over, eyes open and wide as they peered at me through the data fog. "They're trying to *talk* to them."

I had to forcibly stop myself from waving my own eyes in frustrated reply, and instead said, "Who? What are you talking about?"

His mouth flapped a few times, words caught in a tumbling bottleneck at his throat, before he spat out, "The goddamn sentries are sending comms signals *to Fleet scouts*!"

I sprang to my feet, upending the dessert cart behind me with a crash. "FUCKING *WHAT?!*"

/|\

"Well?" I paced the room, head repeatedly snapping toward Bart's form as he moved through the data from the previous two months' scouting engagements, despite my best efforts to give him time to work.

"Yes," he said. "But much less than March, I think. Definitely much less in January, I need to look at February some more."

"It's definitely comms traffic? Not just a feeling?"

He dropped his arms, body language shrouded in holographic mist but still distinctly peeved. "Of *course* it's a feeling, that's how my scrying works, you know that."

I squirmed with restlessness, but said, "I know. I'm sorry."

"Look, I don't know how to explain it to you, but please just trust me. It may as well be like asking me the difference between touching paper and touching ice every time one of them sends out a ping."

"A ping? Not words?"

"Uh ... yeah, I'm not sure this is vocal traffic. Maybe not even data traffic." He grumbled with frustration. "I wish these were *actual* comms records, not astronomy data. Or that they'd allowed any of us Scries into the OC this month instead of furloughing us again, so I'd have some idea of the exact time stamps when AVOC was transmitting ..."

"You *were* there for the January scouting engagement," I pointed out.

"Well, yeah, but I didn't notice anything unusual at all. Probably because they only spent a couple minutes pinging those two scouts, wouldn't even have been enough time for me to spot the movement unless I was already surveying local space at the time. It's ... strange that *no* other Scries noticed it and included it in their report though, now that I think about it. We're supposed to be maintaining whole-Vector surveillance."

"Indeed ..." I replied.

"Anyhow, I can feel the exact same *type* of energy coming from the OC, up to the Corps sentries at certain points before the scouts arrived, and sometimes back down to the planet from the sentries ... and it's in a totally different shape than what I'm feeling from the sentries once the engagement starts. Weaker, or ... or spread out more. Bigger, longer ... enough time to have full conversations. I'm pretty confident I'm detecting the usual pre-engagement radio chatter, there; they use semi-shaping transmitters, and that's exactly what I'd imagine them feeling like in this type of dataset." He lifted his arms again, examining the engagement data one last time before nodding in confirmation. "But these are just blasts. Short, hard blasts of *very* directional comms signal, whatever might be embedded in that signal or not ... Pings. They're pinging the damn scouts. That's what this feels like, I can't think of a better word."

"We've had the January and February scouting data for nearly three weeks now, why haven't you ever noticed this before? And are we sure there was no suspicious activity in Stellary? January was the start?"

He deactivated the desk's display and bent immediately to give it a tender kiss. "Because my baby lets me touch even the weakest trace now," he cooed. "And yeah, pretty sure."

I waved my eyes upward and snorted. "Alright. Investment well made, then."

    Tiny Planet Filled With Liars

"Yes, yes it was, yes it really really was," he murmured lovingly to a circuitry drawer.

"I'm going to be ill if you don't sit down right this second and finish your dinner—AT the table, thank you. That braise is ice cold now, your fault. Once you're done, we need to start comparing this activity with incursion data. Jupiter above."

He gave me a jaunty wink, high on scry, but obediently sat down to eat properly.

/|\

We'd just about finished the most urgent sensor investigations by (a very late) dinner the following day, but I felt no closer to a useful conclusion as I picked sullenly at my pilav in the dining room. It was already quite clear that the entire military had been ordered to stop cooperating with me—COAT be damned—and the dozens of fruitless contacts I'd attempted to make that day while Bart was working had proved the point further. I wasn't even getting return calls from the staff of junior Board members anymore. Unprecedented, given how eager those offices usually are to hear out even the *potential* of a (purportedly) press-related opportunity, even if only for the status-boosting thrill of rejecting it while telling everybody they'd done so. But obviously the word was out about my enterprise, and now I was left paying the political price, despite the prices Zhou and I had already paid. This meant the onus was on me to pursue legal action against genuinely uncooperative subjects, but it would have taken weeks to even schedule a court appearance, and I'd have been lucky to force any interviews at all before the year was out.

Sometimes I really hate this world.

As Bart inhaled a pasty, I reviewed what we now knew, step by step.

"So. In end January, for the first time, 4th sentries direct highly focused comms signals at Fleet scouts."

Bart tried murmuring through a full mouth, then crumbed out, "But just a couple."

I threw a napkin at him. "Yes, just a couple. And only four bursts—or at least four, that we're able to detect."

Bart "mm"ed.

"The location of the two scouts they pinged ..." I sighed. "... do correspond to a region in the Corps formation that's largely occupied by 4th units during incursion, but nearly at the middle of the forward line, while the only operational deficiency we can detect in February's incursion data is still at the left flank hinge point."

"I don't know if you should put that last bit in your report, I still think the fact that I can *barely* detect a TDNF in the February incursion means I might be imagining it. We need more data, or a lot more Scries with military experience taking a look at it. Though even civilian scryers might do, with enough of them to make it empirical."

I shrugged. "We're not building a court case here, just examining our analysis. The data will be there for anybody who wants it. I think the circumstances of what we've otherwise learned give more weight to tentative conclusions in that direction, for now. Though ... I do wish we could get *any* kind of useful locational readings on the squadron that was destroyed that month."

I knew understanding February's incursion probably wasn't the most important missing piece in our puzzle any longer, but I couldn't stop Abby's face from flashing through my mind every time we discussed the first mass casualty event. I fully admit I was hoping to assuage some guilt by providing her and Jieun with answers about Caio's end—COAT be damned—though it was only by presumption that I hoped she'd find it comforting to begin with.

Anyhow.

     TINY PLANET FILLED WITH LIARS

"Activity ramps up significantly in the end February scouting engage-ment, as I witnessed firsthand. Now we know the 'feinting' I observed was actually a ping maneuver, at least in every such instance we've ana-lyzed ..." I shook my head. If only I'd known that in the moment, we might be so much closer to the real facts of the situation now.

I began pouring myself a drink. "February's ping activity does corre-late a little more with the left flank, even considering how many more scouts they pinged that time around ... but only by twenty to thirty per-cent, which I'd say—"

"Ch-ten," Bart said around a mouthful.

I waved my eyes. "Ten to twenty, then. Which I still think is more than enough to call a genuine correlation with the location of the disas-ter in March's incursion, at a minimum." I lifted my glass and swallowed heavily. "But only correlation. We need more."

He nodded in agreement and we lapsed into silence for a time.

While Bart fantasized about which demo dataset he'd play with on the Mk3 after dinner, my thoughts had begun clustering around the source-point of my silently pounding heartbeat, and a dawning fear which I couldn't yet bring myself to confront openly. It wasn't the fact that we didn't know why Vanderbilt's conspirators were so intent on dis-obeying engagement protocols. No.

It was that said conspirators had pinged approximately fifty Fleet scouts prior to an incursion that resulted in nearly 20,000 deaths and the loss of a bulwark; and two days ago they had done the same thing to nearly 300 vessels instead, approaching scouts across every single quad-rant of the Vector.

The April incursion was then five days away.

29

Lieutenant (Junior Grade) Naomlo Kekoa

Alpha Vector Defense Corps Detention Ct. IV, Level 195, Legal Anteroom

[Naomlo Kekoa]

Welp.

[Interviewer]

Welcome back to the closet.

[Naomlo Kekoa]

Least we know how to fuckin' fit in now, I guess.

[Interviewer]

Like puzzle pieces. I believe it's a little easier when I sit down first, we'll try to remember that.

[N.K.]

See the fuckers put a proper window in, too.

[Int.]

Mm. Even better for purposes of—

[N.K.]

...

...

...

Uh. What the shit was *that*?

[Int.]

Mind your fucking business, is what that.

[N.K.]

Whoa, my mistake, didn't mean any offense.

[Int.]

(chuckles) No, sorry. Look.

[N.K.]

...

...

...

Ohhh. Hey I didn't even know any of those were still around any-more. Musta been pricey as shit! Or you killed someone for it. (laughs)
SEE THAT, BEN? CAN'T HEAR SHIT NOW, CAN YOU? FUCK YOU BEN!

...

Oh, fuck. Wait.

...

(mouthing) Fuuuck Yooou.

...

(laughs) He gets it.

...

(laughs) Look they're panicking. Running off to tell paps the snooper's not working, I'm sure.

[Int.]

In all likelihood, but I left a pile of pre-filled, pre-stamped protest forms sticking out of my bag in security. COAT, uh ... long-form, so each one requires additional paperwork from the recipient before they even start processing. I doubt they'll bother us today. Shall we begin?

[N.K.]

Yeah ... I donno. Hear you fuckin' lied to me.

[Int.]

I'm sorry?

[N.K.]

You told me you weren't military.

[Int.]

Ah, I see. I am not. They threw me out some time ago, as it happens.

[N.K.]

Oh yeah? No shit.

...

Why?

...

[scraping chair]

[N.K.]

...

Ohhh. No *shit*, really?

[Int.]

Yes.

[N.K.]

Well goddamn.

...

(laughs)

Guess that explains the accent, then.

[Int.]

Oh my god.

[N.K.]

(raucous laughter)

...

...

...

Ahhh, that's good.

(chuckles)

Alright. You know I'm glad for the company around here, but I don't know what the fuck else I can tell ya. I'm just a mid-low officer, no secrets here.

[Int.]

I've suddenly begun encountering extensive administrative delays in requesting even the most basic demographic statistics from the Corps. I—

...

To be perfectly fucking frank, I'm getting blocked, hard, and I'm spinning my goddamn gears, and I'm pretty sure something terrible is in the works, and I'm just desperate for any cooperative source of any kind for *any* information right now. The fact that you know nothing is probably the only reason they're still voluntarily letting me in the building, I am very aware.

[N.K.]

...

Wow.

[Int.]

Yes.

(sighs)

   Tiny Planet Filled With Liars

In any case, I know there's a limit to your scope of knowledge, but I'd simply like to hear more about your experience in the Corps. Perhaps more has changed since the days of my enlistment than I realize.

[N.K.]

Alright, proud to do my patriotic duty, then. I'll blow ALL the goddamn secrets!

(chuckles)

Everything we get up to while saving the world. The whole batch. Eat, wank, yell; eat, sleep, yell; wank, wank, eat; fuck, fight, sleep— fuckin' finely lubricated machine around here.

(laughs)

[Int.]

Indeed. I sense a new Corps anthem in the offing.

[N.K.]

(raucous laughter)

[Int.]

...

Before we get to other questions, I do have some follow-up on the last incursion. Give me ... uh ... a moment to find the file displays here ... please.

...

[N.K.]

(mouthing) Iiiiii aaamm gooing to beeeaat yooouu doooowwwn.

...

Beeeat yooooou fuuuckiiing doooown. Bloody and—

...

No, BEAT. BEAT. BUH, BUH, BUH. BEE-BEE-BEE. BEEEEEEAAT, DAMMIT!

...

...

Fuck, maybe he thinks I'm offering a knobber. YEAH, SURE, WHEN TOAST TURNS BACK TO BREAD YOU ASSHOLE.

...

BEAT! BUH-EAT-UH! YOUR FACE! MY FIST! LOOK!

[Int.]

Lieutenant, please turn back around or I'll be forced to ask you to hang my jacket over the window.

[N.K.]

(grumbles)

...

Sorry. Fuck Ben.

[Int.]

Yes, fuck Ben. This is an image I pulled from the Prime CCIC during the March incursion, which you may—

[N.K.]

Oh fuck, look ma, it's me.
(laughs)

[Int.]

Yes, that is the Martial Horizons 3, right where the flagship's optical processors froze on the blast issuing from your collision with the Fleet vessel.

[N.K.]

(laughs) Holy shit, look you can even see the bulwark starting to breach there in the background. See that? Little bit of purple glowy fucker right there, next to the plasma flare? That's the ablation reactor.

    TINY PLANET FILLED WITH LIARS

[Int.]

Holy shit, you're right.

...

Remarkable timing.

[N.K.]

Thank you very fuckin' much.

[Int.]

(chuckles)

[N.K.]

Anyway, I've seen that plenty of times already.

[Int.]

What? You have?

[N.K.]

Not your capture, I mean. I've seen the local footage, from the other fuckers nearby.

...

The ones that lived, anyway.

[Int.]

...

They told me all data was corrupted, including visual records.

[N.K.]

(laughs) Yeah, okay, sure. The entire fuckin' fleet. Right.

[Int.]

(sighs) Yes, I know.

...

In what context was it shown to you? The footage, I mean.

[N.K.]

Hearings, in't it? Fuck.ing. constant.

[Int.]

Ah, of course. I imagine you've got one scheduled nearly every day.

[N.K.]

Who knows, they don't even let me go to half of 'em, and I don't care, I sleep better in my *own* cell bed anyway, fuckers.

...

But they've shown that shit to me a lot. Most of the first week they was trying to blame us for the entire damn thing. Like, because I made the FHG so powerful, it was *too good* at slipping energy during the collision and other ships got caught in our backsplash or something.

(snorts)

Fuckin' idiots. Are they even qualified to discuss physics? Sure as shit in't no engineers on those steps. Fuckin' morons. Like, oh, no, I'm sorry, it wasn't the *enormous fucking bulwark atomizing itself two dicks away you piece of shit*, I mean right? Watch, they'll try and say the bulwark going up is my fault too before the end of this.

...

IF I COULD DO ALL THAT WITH A BIT OF FUCKIN' FIELD HARDENING WHY DO WE EVEN BOTHER MAKING FUCKING GUNS, HUH? WHO NEEDS 'EM? FUCK!

...

I mean, goddamn. Right? Goddamn right.

...

...

...

Anyway, yeah I seen it.

(laughs)

    Tiny Planet Filled With Liars

[Int.]

...

Are you worried that your career is over?

[N.K.]

(laughs)

Uh, no. What makes you think there's any question? Hate to break the news to you, but they threw me in prison. Retirement odds not exactly trending up here, are they? Fuck. The worry is over.

[Int.]

You've still got a trial of some sort ahead, nothing's stamped in alloy yet.

[N.K.]

(snorts) Yeah, okay. They're trying to do me in for *not giving me orders to save us*. Come on. Appreciate it, but come on.

(chuckles)

[Int.]

(sighs)

[N.K.]

Anyway, no need to ask which way the rains are gonna fall, they've already given up the game just by the way they talk about all that.

[Int.]

What do you mean?

[N.K.]

Well, fuck, am I a DO here, fuckers, or in't I a goddamn *DO?!*

...

Does that fucking picture not show an *intact* goddamn laser boat gettin' the shit kicked out of it? Right? A fucking *defended* goddamn laser boat?

...

Not a cloud of fucking glowing dust and blood powder.

...

But here I am. So case closed. I don't need to be told twice.

[Int.]

...

...

...

Why did you decide to enlist, originally? Obviously you don't fit the usual overeager profile.

[N.K.]

Damn, you really are older than you look, huh?

[Int.]

(chuckles) I guess so.

[N.K.]

Nobody enlists because they wanna go parading the banner around anymore. You enlist because the fuckin' fuckers're gonna get you anyway, so may as well do it first and snag a shorter term. Or at least, that's how it was a few years ago.

[Int.]

Ah ... I wonder how contemporary intake levels compare to the average in my day.

[N.K.]

Well, either not fuckin' great, or they're planning a whole new fleet lately.

     TINY PLANET FILLED WITH LIARS

[Int.]

What?

[N.K.]

Recruitment levels. Like, back in your day there was probably, what, fifty-fifty split between recruitments and enlistments? Right?

[Int.]

Yes, that's probably roughly accurate.

[N.K.]

Well, fuck. There you go. Even when I enlisted it was probably still about sixty-forty. That was what, five? Six years ago? Curlies practically still fresh in my pants then, fuck.
(laughs)

…

But anyway, just a couple months ago I was reading that recruitment indentures were about to hit 80 percent of intake.

[Int.]

What?!

…

Holy shit.

…

Eighty fucking percent indenture.

[N.K.]

Yeah. Goddamn worst part is everybody knows it's totally fucking unnecessary.

[Int.]

How so?

[N.K.]

Well, they'd probably get by on a third of the number, if they wanted to, right? Us meatbags are just the cheap, expendable shit you litter all over the fuckin' place to prove that you need more fucking money in the budget next quarter to clean up after us.

…

Fuckers got smart to folks enlisting to minimize their time, so they jacked up minimum enlistment terms. Now, more people figure why the fuck bother? They'll get us anyway, so enjoy the time while you can, wait for the fuckers to hafta come knocking on your door.

…

Suppose eventually they'll do the reverse, start indenturing people for ten more years on top, and people will have to start enlisting more often to avoid it, soon as they get any hint they're in the doom funnel.

[Int.]

…

Or the Corps will just start indenturing for life again.

[N.K.]

…

…

Fuck. Yeah that scries, don't it.

…

Fuckers.

[Int.]

Indeed.

   Tiny Planet Filled With Liars

[N.K.]

They're probably gonna have to anyway, once word gets out about all this shit.

[Int.]

Mm.

[N.K.]

Question number fucking one at drill will start being, "Why the fuck you fucking fuckers sitting here telling us we don't need to train for dynamic fucking combat scenarios? WE SEEN THE FUCKING VIDS, IDIOTS!"
(laughs)
All their "Push Button A at Time Interval four-five-dot-four and repeat indefinitely" bullshit. How about "dodge the electric arc that just shitting crisped your goddamn buddy and reset the fuckin' deck breaker which I hope you fuckin' know how to do because the goddamn blaze responder is five fucking decks away and you DON'T KNOW HOW TO DO ANYTHING BUT PUSH FUCKING BUTTONS AND OH LOOK A FIREBALL JUST REDECORATED YOUR FUCKIN' WORKSTATION!"
(pants)
Fuck.
...
Those fuckin' turds are gonna start really regretting that most of us in't trained for actual fucking combat, just Standing Orders assembly line bullshit ... if they keep up like this. No goddamn wonder they wanna do me in for having a thought. Fuck.

[Int.]

...

...

I suppose my own service perspective was more ... um, academic. Perhaps I should have started speaking with more lower level officers and other personnel immediately, when it came to these Certs.

[N.K.]

(laughs) Ya fuckin' think?

[Int.]

Fair.

[N.K.]

Tell you what'll really send the shit skyward, though. Once the families find out.

[Int.]

Oh?

[N.K.]

Uh, yeah. And not even the dead ones' either—that's a *whole other* bomb waitin'a go.

...

You think the average ass walking down the street even knows what *happens* during an incursion? Think some random pleb gives more than two shittin' thoughts to Fleet their entire lives?

[Int.]

Well—

[N.K.]

Sure, sure. It's an exaggeration, in't it? But not *that* much.

...

My family has *no fucking idea* I'm sitting up there every month trying to stop myself getting boiled alive in bulwark spilloff, do they? You kidding?

     Tiny Planet Filled With Liars

...

The fuck do they know about it except what shows up in flix now
and then, or the evening reports nobody but goddamn sleeping
old whitehairs watch anyway? It's fuckin' fireworks to them, in't
it? Not fighting.

[Int.]

Valid point.

[N.K.]

Just wait'll you hear the fucking scream when THAT bandage gets
ripped off.

...

(laughs) Oh I hope I'm still here to hear it.

...

'Course, with the way they vom' up new classifications every other
week these days, who the shit knows. Maybe nobody'll ever find
out what happened to any of us. Poor fuckers at home just have to
be like "well it's been thirty fucker fucking years, guess they dead,
hope they send the corpse sometime so I can fuckin' kiss it goodbye."

...

(laughs) I'm sure the fuckers'll make it public right after they tell
everyone where them new drive shapers suddenly appeared from.

[Int.]

...

...

...

What?

[N.K.]

You know, on the corvettes. New shapers suddenly started gettin'
manufactured few years ago, fuckin' plus twenty up maneuver-
ability or some bullshit. Outta nowhere. Craziness. Wegnerite
Complex got the contract, but it was goin' around the whispers
immediately. Number one because Wegnerite's run by morons,
right? Can't even make a shitter that don't burst into flames, or
crack in two soon as your ass hits it.

...

(laughs) In't no way they developed *that* shit.

[Int.]

Wait, what was going around? What are you talking about?

[N.K.]

(huffs)
You did fuckin' say you've been investigating, right? Fuck.

...

The *drive shapers*! How they came from salvage, goddamn. Or the
design, anyway—Fleet torp' propulsion or something. That wa—

[audible impact, scraping]

[N.K.] (simultaneous)

(explosive exhale)
ooOWW-UH! DAMN!

[Int.] (simultaneous)

What the *fuck did YOU JUST SAY*?

...

Oh my god, are you okay?

[audible scraping]

  TINY PLANET FILLED WITH LIARS

[N.K.]

(chuckles) Fuck, warn me to suck it in next time you're gonna stand up like that. Goddamn.

[Int.]

I'm so sorry. This fucking table edge is a—are you sure you're okay?

[N.K.]

Let's fuckin' hope not, right? Hope you busted a goddamn kidney, they'll have to take me to a real hospital and I can whine my way into gettin' a new hand finally.
(laughs)
Fuck.

[Int.]

I'm so sorry. What can—

...

I need an interview immediately with whoever you heard this from. (muttering) Three more days ... is that even enough time?

[N.K.]

Sure, have it, but you'll have a hard time finding 'em, their missile cruiser took it in the bulwark blast. But if you're up for interviewing some goddamn dust ...
(laughs)
Ow that hurts—hey, maybe my luck is takin' a fucking turn!

30

YOU'VE SEEN the same reports I have. Day in, day out.

Over, and over.

And over. The same clips.

First that shot—the one from the bank feed. Bird sitting on the ledge, preening. What's that in the background? Is that a raindrop on the scope? No, it's the clouds? Bird flies away. Cloud starts to boil.

Or the other one, couple on a vid call with family across the world, in the park. Picnic, maybe, we never get to see what's in front of them. Just that sudden brightening when they're talking about some kind of party, and they look up—the one's hat falls off, and then the grass starts to singe underneath them and the feed cuts.

Or maybe that one with the asshole reporter, you know the one, doing some walk-n-talk in that underpass, and he starts screaming at the lighting tech when the sky behind them starts to bloom out and go white, like it's their fault ... and that stupid hair instantly going flat in the downdraft when he steps out from under the bridge ...

You know, the old classics.

And then they all start to look the same, don't they? All the angles. Just ... white. Blown out opticals. Sometimes screams on the audio still, for a few seconds, but usually not. Usually just that roar ...

You have to move three districts away until you get a good angle on what's actually happening. The stadium feed, right? That's where we all saw it the first time. Live. When the feeds inside the zone had cut. That's when the anchors all switched and we knew what was really happening. That pillar of boiling white. Hard to even pick out, until you realize it's the entire sky. Until you realize those mountains at its edge are *behind* it, hundreds of kilometers away.

AVDC scientists will probably spend decades crawling over every reading they can get their hands on, trying to figure out what that beam even *is*, never mind how it works. I've seen a few reports already. Incomprehensible. Such densely woven energy patterns ... in honesty, it's hard for me to believe *they* even believe it's real. It must be a scrying error, right? It can't possibly really be like that behind the edge. Bartimus refuses to examine the data even now, nearly a week later; says he doesn't want it inside his head again, after having to endure it at AVOC that day.

But of course on the feeds, in our lives, it's not complex at all, is it?

Just a solid sheet of white; dirt to sky. Burns the eyes to look at, even through opticals. Featureless, except where dust, or smoke, or vaporized ... billowing around it, glowing from behind, and then you start to see buildings disappearing *into* it ... in one feed, Palace Naverbok, even ... crumbling like crackers ...

And then it's gone. And if the feed you're watching still has audio, you can hear the birds start wailing immediately, and the horizon is already gone spiky with the ground emplacements firing into orbit, long condensation tracers up through the shockwave ripples. And their rounds are already vanished up into the black beyond the blue by the time they start popping in your ears ...

And then it's just that crater. Just the zone. Still glowing and livid, then. Not ash and ink, like now.

And then you think, well thank Jupiter, it must've only been a few blocks. What could have happened?

But the perspective is off in that mountain range. It tricks the eye, the way those ridges wander back and forth, especially on camera from that far away. You have to read or watch other reports to find out it's really seven full districts. Nearly eight, with the pieces of the others that got caught near the edge.

And then you get a call from Abby and Jieun. And you suddenly realize 61 is on the list, even though you've been looking at it *constantly, godammit why didn't I*; but they're okay, thank Jupiter, they were shopping and dinner over in this quadrant that afternoon and remembered you lived around here and can they stay? Of course, of course, come, please, now, my security will meet you at the shuttle station, I have an entire empty wing, please, hurry, I heard the debris cloud is only a few hours away, they'll shut the sub-orbital lanes soon ...

And I know.

I know.

I know that for many of you this marks the first day you've joined our tale, in your own minds. The first time you bothered looking up from your own lives to notice the scenery coming to pieces around you.

I know.

I resent you. I hold it against you. I require you to make compensation throughout your days. I demand it. I *will* wield these Certs in coercion of you, if needs must, and your culpability requires. For godsake, if even *I* could see ...

You may not have had my money, or my network of contacts, but you had *eyes*, just as I have eyes. You should not have needed to *wait* for my words—they are incomplete, and paid for, and as much truth as not! A world should not hang from them! I am not strong enough to bear such cords! Nobody is.

YOU HAD MY EYES.

...

So I forgive you. How could I possibly not?

You might have been thrown in prison for trying to turn fact into truth, I know that. Have I not paid billions to waylay just such a fate for us all now? I know.

But you've seen what a flaccid shell COAT has become. I admit this is also known.

I admit this is known.

I admit.

Is your life not worth more to you, even inside the sheltering womb of your own skull? More than rules that were already broken by the masters who set them aside before you limped up to place their burden on your own broken back instead?

Is mine?

I wonder. I feel a fiction inside myself beginning to crack.

Some consequences are too unforgivable to bear.

Now you exist in this world. Now your eyes live here, too. They ought to have sooner. Much sooner.

Why didn't they?

But I don't blame you.

After all;

Everybody's got rent to pay, even when they own.

There are only so many hours in a day.

So many days in a week.

So many years in a life.

Too few now, for too many.

I know there would be some several more among your number here, reading alongside us. Desperate. Terrified. Praying for information. Feeling the span toward the next incursion move like the pulse in your jaw.

TINY PLANET FILLED WITH LIARS

More of you, for certain.

But unfortunately many of you have lately become cinders.

And cinders don't read.

31

2nd Division "Bulwark" Command Prime
(Alpha Vector), Deck 54,
Command Combat Information Center

[rumbling and other distortion throughout transcript]

[Admiral]

The light's on?

[Scry 1]

Yes.

[Admiral]

The moment I call stand down, turn it off and hand it back to me then never mention this again.

[Scry 1]

Aye, sir.

[audible explosion]

[Rear Admiral]

AVOC is launching the entire SAR fleet now. And new east escort should be here soon, looks like we'll need that screen after all.

[Admiral]

Mm. Probably should've let ours stay, I don't think they'll catch up in time. Hope they're at least popping snipe on the way.

[Rear Admiral](simultaneous)

I'm sure.

[Scry 1](simultaneous)

Marker six, FAILURE!

[Rear Admiral]

Downhill where?

[Admiral]

There's no downhill here. Look at those bloom deviations—what the *fuck* is Fleet doing today?

[Rear Admiral]

What the fuck down *there*?

[Admiral](simultaneous)

I know. Building something?

[Rear Admiral](simultaneous)

I'm starting to think—

[Admiral]

I know, Jon. The fastest way out of this is still reset. DD is shifting the curves already. But—DD AMEND DD SAFETY FREE. DD SAFETY FREE. CONFIRM.

[Rear Admiral](simultaneous)

The accountants are gonna—

[Tactical 1](simultaneous)

Escort ETA thirty.

[Tactical 2](simultaneous)

DD SAFETY FREE AYE ... CONFIRM!

[Rear Admiral](simultaneous)

Thirty? Tell them to HARD BURN. NOW. How out of position *were* they?

[Tactical 1](simultaneous)

Hard burn, aye.

[Admiral]

Mess of an abort.

[Scry 2]

Marker seven, FAILURE!

[Rear Admiral]

Open main to Commander Bastowitz.

[Communications 1](simultaneous)

Aye, main open.

[audible explosion](simultaneous)

[Rear Admiral]

Lou, tell me you're on the way.

[Commander Bastowitz](transmission)

Jon I don't think we're gonna make it down in time.

[Admiral]

Then make it in time, Louelen. Please.

[Commander Bastowitz](transmission)

Alright, Seersa. Off.

[Rear Admiral]

You think?

[Admiral](simultaneous)

No. Probably ... not.

[Scry 1](simultaneous)

MARKER EIGHT FAILURE. RESET FAILURE.

[Tactical 2]

Oh my god.

[Admiral]

East abort status.

[Tactical 1]

Complete!

[Admiral]

If we hadn't had to in the first place—

[Rear Admiral](simultaneous)

SitCheck.

[Admiral](simultaneous)

Come on, Lou ...

[Scry 1]

Point zero zero eight, CHECK.

[widespread screaming]

[Admiral](simultaneous)

No.

[Operations 1](simultaneous)

Oh my god.

[Scry 2](simultaneous)

Oh my god!

[Communications 1](simultaneous)

THE PLANET!

[audible explosion](simultaneous)

[Rear Admiral]

Where's our FUCKING **ESCORT**?! Should we send more down?

[Admiral](simultaneous)

No. We need reset. Now.

[Communications 1](simultaneous)

FLASH COMM!

[Commander Bastowitz](transmission)

Blew out the diffusers but just about made it, we're going in. Send everything you can after me, Seersa. We won't get a—RAMMING THROTTLE, ARMS FREE! Jupiter above boy, no the ram setting is right THERE ALL UNITS, BRACE FOR COLLISION AND DIVE IN—HIT THE FLAT SIDE! MAX—

(transmission squeal)

[Communications 1](simultaneous)

Dropout.

[Rear Admiral](simultaneous)

Can they clean up in time?

[Admiral]

1st south is right there behind. Maybe.

[Tactical 1]

Ground defense in range of structure, engaged!

[Rear Admiral]

Seersa we won't get another—

[Admiral]

I know—SITCHECK, GI—

[widespread screaming](simultaneous)

[Admiral](simultaneous)

WATCH THE CANOPY!

[explosion, electric distortion, audio blowout]

…

…

…

[seventeen seconds of distortion ringing]

…

…

…

[warning klaxon, distorted]

[Communications 1](distorted)

 … say again, all flee—

 …

 …

 … —wo, one, niner—

 …

 … two, one, nin—

 …

 …

 ACKNOWLEDGE SEND FREQUENCY.

[Operations 1](simultaneous)

 FHG back online.

[Admiral](simultaneous)

 JON!

[Scry 1](simultaneous)

 Oh my god.

[Tactical 2]

Admiral!

[Admiral](simultaneous)

JON!

[Scry 1](simultaneous)

Marker eight-plus-one, COMPLETE!

[Admiral]

CONFIRM SITCHECK. JON!

[Scry 2]

Confirm, point zero one two.

[Operations 1](simultaneous)

Setting Condition Beta, sir. On recognizance.

[Tactical 1](simultaneous)

(weeping)
Disengagement in progress.

[Admiral](simultaneous)

GET THAT FUCKING MED POD UP HERE NOW. JON!

[Tactical 1](simultaneous)

(weeping)
Complete.

[Scry 1]

Stand down conditions. Board is clear.

[Tactical 2](simultaneous)

Confirm. Clear board.

[Operations 2](simultaneous)

(weeping)
Clear board, confirm.

[Admiral]

STAND DOWN. JON! OH GOD, LOOK AT—

[recording ends]

32

Commander Louelen Bastowitz

*UFD Last Chance 6 (Standing Rains Berth 2P),
Deck 18, Commander's Ward Room*

I NOW relay to you an encounter which, until recently, seemed to call for nothing but notation in my databases. While it did precede additional discoveries, my experience at the time was one of only exhausted and apparently inconsequential bewilderment; not worth examining further. However, I've come to grapple with its relevance since, and so convey here my first ever meeting with Commander Louelen Bastowitz the previous month, at the end of March's incursion day.

Despite Kudaibergen's assurances (earlier that day) that I would have plenty of time to introduce myself to the Commander following my hasty post-engagement evacuation from Command Prime, I hadn't actually been able to meet them until we'd already docked at Standing Rains. Instead, I'd endured the entire trip pacing in the docking hall while the plebby run recruits continued to melt down around me with escalating volume. By the time we landed I was already fighting the overload headache which would continue growing throughout that night. My mood was accordingly quite sour, but I forced civility when a nameless Lieutenant pulled me aside from the stream of gibbering recruits, who were spilling from disembarkation in a tumbling pelt toward dry land. Following such rescue, the Lieutenant asked me to accompany him to the Commander's ward room, where Bastowitz had requested a word.

Upon our arrival at the appropriate deck, he directed me toward the Commander's door from the end of the corridor, but returned to the lift immediately while I moved on alone.

The door opened as soon as I approached the threshold, and I was quite surprised by the austerity of the Commander's office space behind it. Surprised because I knew such a spartan layout would have required incessant deflection of attempts to outfit the suite with an array of expensive materials and useless knackery sent by important contractors. Indeed, I knew for a fact that the majority of said contractors would view those bare walls and decking as an insult—even an outright abdication of Bastowitz's duty to the Dominion as a command-level officer.

I would later discover that the truth was even more definitively Bastowitz. They did in fact accept every offer of gifting and renovation raised by a contractor, then simply used the materials and proceeds in other areas of the ship, or shoved them into storage bays at Standing Rains, to be forgotten about while the Commander got on with their work in the preferred and unadorned environment. Clever photography angles and convenient lapses in memory covered the rare occasion when a contractor insisted on direct evidence of their product's presence in the ward room, or was simply desperate for a publicity shot to share with the media.

The Commander was wrapping up a call as the ward room door slid shut behind me, and beckoned to a sharp-angled chair in front of their desk.

"Love you too," they concluded a moment later, before setting the receiver aside and leaning back in their own chair. "Apologies. My husband insists on cooking a special dinner at the end of every incursion, even when I don't feel like requesting anything." Bastowitz shook their eyes a bit, then smiled slightly.

   TINY PLANET FILLED WITH LIARS

"I can't imagine you'll feel much like celebrating this evening," I replied.

Bastowitz shook their head. "No, I do not imagine so."

"Thank you for the … ride. Or whatever this was."

The Commander chuckled dryly. "Whatever this was, indeed."

"I don't … uh, I don't really understand what just happened, I must be honest with you. What was the sudden rush to get me off Command Prime? Why—and what went wrong with the incursion? It nearly failed, didn't it? What's going on here?"

They said only, "Did you have any opportunity to discuss the situation with your fellow passengers?"

I cocked my head in confusion. "The new recruits? Uh … no. We didn't really speak much. They were barely coherent, to be frank." I chuckled. "I know that was quite an experience from the bridge, but I'm surprised they found it so shattering even from a vid feed in a briefing room somewhere."

Bastowitz smiled a little. "Indeed. But as it happens they weren't in a briefing room, they were in the VIP suite."

"Oh … really? I wouldn't have expected a facility like that to be given over to a plebby run."

"It isn't, usually."

"Usually?"

"Seersa had a last minute order to include an OIT from a Prime voting family in the roster, necessitating a change of venue as befits the status of that particular dynasty."

The Commander seemed to study me carefully for any reaction to that statement, but I had none.

"Ah, I see," I said; detecting no particular import at the time.

Bastowitz considered me for a moment longer, then nodded. "So, rather than leave trainees of such status on the ship during SAR, it was decided to bring them back planetside with dispatch."

"Ahhh, I see," I said. "And I just happened to be there too."

"Mm," they replied.

"Although, actually, it was strange, I think I was supposed to be sent back on an orbital skip, but for some reason—"

The Commander suddenly pulled up a navigational playback and interrupted me without preamble. "Yes, considering our passengers we felt obliged to take an express slot back to berthing, as you can see here, so it'll be quite some time before the rest of the fleet arrives home."

I nodded with growing confusion. After processing what I was actually looking at, I pointed to a group of a dozen or so smaller vessels which appeared to be trailing the Commander's sub-unit (us) in the adjacent traffic lane. "I see ... Does your escort unit normally travel with you throughout the day? It's not that I doubt the frivolity of the Corps when it comes to burning through drive reserves like that," I laughed. "But seems they might possibly have been some help with SAR back in the formation, doesn't it? Once the lockdown is lifted, I mean."

"We do not operate with additional escort, and SAR activity does not require additional assistance," Bastowitz replied. Again, they seemed to observe my reaction carefully afterward.

I nodded once more, brow wrinkling. "I see ..."

On the navigational display, an icon tagged as a destroyer abruptly fell out of formation with the Commander's sub-unit and dropped behind. As it did so, it almost appeared to swing around and present its broadside to the not-escorts, which all came to a halt in their own lane shortly afterward, while the Commander's group continued on its way.

"Oh," I said while pointing at the icon, "engine problems?"

   Tiny Planet Filled With Liars

Bastowitz stood. "Forgive my discourtesy, I didn't intend to take up so much of your time. I simply wanted to ensure you've arrived safely and satisfactorily—I hope the combat launch on the shuttle wasn't too arduous. I know they can be rough if you're not still drilling them twice per year."

I laughed and stood in kind, promptly forgetting about the navigational display. "Yeah, you're telling me. Fortunately I'd had a light lunch."

The Commander chuckled and held an arm toward the door. "May I escort you to disembarkation?"

"Please," I said gratefully.

We continued chatting on the way.

"Have you served with the Admiralty long?" I inquired as we stepped onto a cyclic lift.

"Oh, Jon and I drilled together," Bastowitz replied.

"Indeed!" I said with surprise. "How lovely for you, I can't imagine old drill buddies often get to serve together in such close capacity at these ranks."

They nodded. "It has been a pleasure, I won't deny. Jon was my husband's consort-in-proxy at the wedding, and we've known Seersa since she began coming up through the Admiralty about ten years after us."

"Ahhh," I said with new understanding. "A happy family, then."

"Mm," Bastowitz intoned warmly.

As we stepped into the disembarkation area, the Commander offered me a friendly quarter-salute. "You have all your supplies? *All* your equipment?"

I nodded, feet twitching eagerly to get on the ramp. "I do. Thank you very much for the hospitality, and the swift return."

Bastowitz smiled briefly, then nodded in recognition behind me, where I turned to see Mira waiting at the end of the ramp.

"Kindest regards to the Admiralty, as well," I said while bowing my head. "Goodbye, Commander."

"Goodbye."

33

The Interviewer
Pleiades Tower, Penthouse Supreme

MY THOUGHTS return to the bridge of Command Prime, at the end of the March incursion, where Admiral Kudaibergen reaches down to the Communications workstation to provide her genetic authorization, verifying the order to lockdown the entire fleet under Protocol Black. In such manner she attempts to freeze Vanderbilt's conspirators in place, or alternately force them to reveal themselves through unsanctioned movement, even as the shattered corpse of the bulwark spews suffocated fire above them all.

I think of how most genetic authorizations require only a scraping of skin cells from the thumb's surface, but ones of this magnitude mandate complete spectrum tissue sampling, via hollow probe thrust into the inert marrow-producing matrices of the scaphoid bone, deep beneath the fleshy base of the Admiral's right thumb.

I think of the fine spray of blood that mists from the Admiral's hand as she lifts it off the authorization pad.

I think of Smythe, who moves toward a medical cabinet before the word "lockdown" has fully parted the Admiral's lips, and who is silently and diligently applying a bandage to the Admiral's hand even while it returns to her side.

I think of my final view of the Admiralty. My neck is craned behind as babbling recruits jostle me down the boarding ramp, and I catch a last glimpse of Smythe through the blurred heads rushing around me. He is lifting Kudaibergen's hand with urgent concern, muttering, her face awash in fond tolerance of his fussy ministrations as he leans in close and inspects the injury.

I wonder if he'd been standing near the medical cabinet in anticipation of another lockdown when the razor-thin pinwheels of Fleet radiation coming off the exploding lens structure sliced across that bridge with tragic circumstantial precision.

/|\

I don't understand why we can't be better.

I don't understand why it's so hard to stop getting worse.

I don't understand why we must begin dying before we can change.

I am tired of being part of this world alone.

I find myself wondering why so many of these Board members are so incredibly greedy, beyond all bounds of what comfort or power any person might possibly make use of in the span of a life. Their villainy is almost beyond belief, except that it happens in front of our very eyes; day, to month, to year, to century. Whenever it seems they've improved, one inevitably discovers they've only erected a more effective camouflage for their perfidy. They make it so hard to advocate for their rule, even as I yearn to let go of my cares ...

They have to do *so little* to meet the barest requirements of their rank and responsibility, and yet they refuse. It starts to become clear that this is a deliberate choice, an announcement that they exist above, beyond, not of our world.

And yet they *are* of our world, and their mistakes are ours, and our deaths are ours as well.

I find myself wondering, for the first genuine time, if my core faith in the ability of this common system to provide for its own continuation is

 TINY PLANET FILLED WITH LIARS

really so certain, and if not, what comes after it? Every day I seem to lose a little more belief, and I do not know where I will be when I bring myself to open my eyes again tomorrow.

I find myself resenting these pathetic scions of the universe. I compare my sacrifices to theirs. How many countless hours have I dedicated to this pursuit of fact? Have I not littered this text with embarrassing details about my personage, purely in forthcoming cultivation of a soil conducive to truth? Have I not literally *taken a knife to the back* in defense of it all? For some semblance of actual reality, as we all experience it? To give you the *truth* of my mind as I reveal facts of this world? Have I not expended, and had expended on my behalf, billions just to chase their lies?

Why can't they say a single thing that's not a goddamn lie?

And this isn't even the start.

You can see in my databases for yourself. Five hundred eighty three rejected, deflected, suspended, or ignored queries submitted in good and proper order. Two hundred thirty three refusals of interview requests. Thousands of unanswered initial contacts, even before the military erected its firewall against me.

Here, allow me to assemble for you a summary of all such responses from several different letters, from several different units, and several different Board offices—representative in every possible way:

(**Dear**)(*plebs*), (ᵂᵉ)(ᵣₑₛₚₑ𝒸ₜfᵤₗₗy)(*decline*), (***eat***)(shit), (*sincerely*) yours.

And how many countless hours of pointless stonewalling transcripts, from the lowest depths of bureaucracy to the highest ranks of leadership?

I strike with the force of *their law*. And even so. A pittance of cooperation.

What recourse is left to me?

Of course, the consequence of my truths is but the wealth and fame of a lifetime, while they wield the power of entire civilizations. I can see how the incentive structure might differ.

I have come to fear that the existence of this structure is in itself an unforgivable mistake which we shall rue for generations.

You want me to say there's some deeper level of machination here, and there is—but it's a matter of degree, not a change in conclusory destination. This is not about a scheme; it is about the shape of a landscape built collectively by ourselves, and which, having been built at all (and with the bitter nostalgia for home we grant to even the lowliest parcel as long as it holds a roof to keep us dry), we cannot now bring ourselves to truthfully describe even in our own minds, for fear of making it unbearable to live there still.

But we must describe it in order to continue living at all, now.

Kudaibergen's motives, I believe, are clear. She has saved us, and may very well save us again. And yet she is culpable.

The landscape she moves within tells her to play games with our lives in perceived pursuit of greater good. Tells her the only way out is through, even when our corpses pave the trail she must walk to get there. Tells her there's no point leaving that trail, even though she might set a foot outside its bounds on occasion. Tells her doing any more is, in fact, forbidden, on threat of utter ostracization. Tells her the world *depends* on her presence on that trail, in order to save us from even worse; and even as that worse comes and comes again, despite her willing obeisance before it. She dare not stray.

Smythe, Bastowitz, and many others, they walked this trail as well. All. Knowingly.

Such is this landscape.

My own motives, I believe, are clear. And yet I am culpable.

I look back on the earliest entries in this report—written before I understood even the possibility of what was to come—and acknowledge my motives at *that* time. I am still in fidelity with those desires now. I admit it.

For notoriety. For fame. For the agency of my own treasure, and for its ability to move me through this world unbound.

For revenge. Revenge on a system which ought to have protected me from attack, and now refuses to protect even *us*.

Revenge wrought by the system's own tools; to prove their worth; to prove they can be wielded correctly; to prove we're not dying for nothing out here. A multifunction blow struck against the vacuum itself.

Elegant in its calculated impotence.

I have known the trajectory of these incursion catastrophes from the very first weeks, but even as such weeks pile up I still feel obligated to be able to further "prove" that trajectory before it is debuted to you. Prove to *whose* standards? The dead? I don't know. But I'm fairly certain they care less about this than the rest of us need to. In fact I'd be willing to bet they no longer require convincing at all, wouldn't you say?

I don't know.

Even now.

Such is this landscape.

And yet, where once those motives were only *supported* by a secondary urge, the analysis ratios have flipped, and now what was afterthought has taken primacy inside my bones. It urges me to lift my legs and plant my feet anew.

I understand now that I walk a landscape where many of those who've paid for the breeds of eyes and mouths that can move worlds instead walk through ours with those selfsame tools insistently shut. They do this because they don't believe we deserve the acknowledgment of their senses, much less their efforts on our behalf. Our very existence in the landscape is a necessary but unpleasant affront. It reminds them of the withered and betrodden shadows of obligation that still stubbornly cling to them, even in their splendor. They desire nothing more than the moments when they might peek a lid open whilst nose to nose with another of their own breed, and so live inside the only shared world they care to contemplate. A perfectly blissful closed circuit.

Zhou was correct, again.

I understand now that my willingness to come to you with mouth and eyes open, and working, gives me power that nobody else seems capable of exercising in this moment, throughout the entire Dominion.

I have paid for this burden and this power, and I acknowledge the duty it gives to me on this day.

A duty to myself, but *more* importantly a duty to you. And I know you understand me well enough by now to know what it fucking means when I say *that* shit, you hear me?

So I hope you strapped in at the start. I'm sorry it took me so long to get here.

I've known from the day I purchased the first Cert that I confronted a high likelihood of failure at the moment of final decision. An inevitable filibuster. From the very first meeting with my publishers, they made it clear that they did not consider it reasonable to complete even a basic legal review in anything less than a year's time—from the point of *first* draft! They argued quite stridently that to do any less was to imperil the careers of everybody involved, plus their family members. I quite concur.

They don't understand the imperative to reveal. To release. To shine light. And I don't feel obliged to convince them of it.

In a world where we're dying because most of you believe a lie, it is a duty to unite the warring realities with fact, and so give people the honest chance to understand what is happening just outside their range of

   TINY PLANET FILLED WITH LIARS

view. Even when they need it shoved into their faces if they're to see clearly.

Those who shirk such duty have ensured that all blood lost is theirs to bear. The vacuum of facts is a garden for suicidal self-deception. There is no plausible excuse or possible alternate result to foresee from the enforced ignorance of those who might otherwise help us fight back to save their own lives, and those of their families, if only they knew the true threat moving overhead. There was never any excuse, but even the phony claim to ignorance of outcome is dead now.

Those with the ability to inform must act swiftly.

A crime such as that undertaken by Kudaibergen and myself can only be repaid with atonement by action. For the rest of our days. Ceaselessly.

Others have already paid the ultimate price for their own abdications; good-hearted and well-intentioned as they may *ever* have been, or not.

I will not bear more blood than I already have. I refuse, and any person of any conscience at all would do the same in my position. I will not regret this decision, whatever my publishers may believe.

However, their lawyers were quite loyal in my regard throughout the investigatory process, and I have no complaints as to my treatment during our contracted tenure. I appreciate the (obscenely expensive) services of all involved with utmost sincerity.

But I *will* turn fact into truth. Here; and now.

We have just under three weeks until the Athra incursion. And thirty days later, the May incursion. And June. And on and on. It will be a first summer of blood, and we'll be lucky to see second summer at all. You think the panicked rioting over the munitions complex was upsetting? That was only half of a single defense factory, we're *lucky* the beam was primarily centered on residential districts! Ponder *that* horror. What if Standing Rains or one of the secondary berthing installations happen to be squarely in view of the next lens attack? We don't even have the abil-

ity to land most of these combat ships elsewhere, and the only maintenance facilities in orbit are for the bulwarks! And what of the rest of us
in the meanwhile? How many times do you think we can lose millions in
a day, before there are no millions left to lose? Already the seismic anom-
alies around the zone point to the fate of our world's crust if it endures
many more such blows. This is insanity.

Vanderbilt must be stopped, and those with the legal power to do so
are bound by their duty to act. Our cowardice will never be forgot otherwise. We shall exist solely and rightfully in infamy, and so have but one
choice before us:

Be redeemed; or not.

I know it.

I should have published sooner. I understand now.

I have exercised the termination clause of my publishing contract and
gladly paid the coterie slaughter fee. I have applied an aggressively trans-
parent stance in my declassification of materials, and include all such
data in my public nets. I also include the entirety of this summary report, free to the public, though I have partnered with an independent
distributor to ensure the book archive will be available via the usual
wholesale and retail channels.

I waive all discretionary claims to Cert monopoly over the topic of
these incursions, and the role played by the military and Board in their
outcomes. I clear all rights to other journalism, analysis, and investigation—registered and civilian—and authorize any citizen of the Dominion who has read this report to wield the rhetorical freedom attendant
to that fact, from COAT, via {*SUC.171, Alpha, amended*}, in perpetu-
ity. However, I *must* be credited in all such representations as the author
of this report and source of this data. I retain all other revenue generat-
ing rights and intellectual ownership assertions for my own work,
present and future, but not work generated from my raw data by the

labors of others. You can find the pre-filled levy exemption paperwork on file with COAT. Use it as you will; it is admissible in legal proceedings without my further intervention.

You see how goddamn serious I am.

I claim the *inalienable* right to take the course of action described in all of the above, and in my court filings of mid-April, as buttressed and *demanded* by the entirety of the Applied Thought provisions of the System Unified Code.

Disputes may be directed to the lawyers on record, *thank you*.

I choose to depart from this trail, and I now put my career in your hands accordingly. I do so because I firmly believe that the trail will be a crater soon if I do not.

Give me a bag of bills big enough to set me up for life, and I promise to reveal to you every important secret I find along the way.

The core lie is simple. It is the very idea that the entire framework of the Board, the military, and even the Presidency itself has much concern for your safety at all. Yet that is the bargain you negotiate, is it not? That is the wellspring of your complacency. The agreement you strike with your masters. For safety, quiescence. For survival, assent. The barest minimum mandate.

To say so isn't outlandish. The outlandish idea is that we could ever rely on a handful of bloodline dunces to run our world to begin with. We've made a terrible error.

These empty fucking sacks can't even wipe their own filthy holes without a mirror.

Trust me.

It's time to grow up. It's time to stop being very tall fucking useless stupid babies and take responsibility for our own world. I call on you to do so alongside me.

This Board has allowed the likes of Crowley Vanderbilt to become ascendant. To move the Dominion of his own volition, and to do it without our consent. We have already paid the toll for that failure, and will pay yet more before we are through.

Such is now scribed into the very dirt of this landscape forevermore.

If they can't even keep you safe, what do you owe them? Nothing.

You owe them **nothing**.

But you are owed.

You are owed a blood price.

You are owed a blood price.

YOU ARE OWED A BLOOD PRICE.

GLORY TO THE RETURNS

 Tiny Planet Filled With Liars

INTERLUDE

34

[Board Advocate]

And when you were given that order, did you believe it was a timely one?

[Accused Advocate]

Excuse me—

[Board Advocate](simultaneous)

(huffs) Your Eminence—

[Adjudicator](simultaneous)

Esteemed Fellows, I will not Warn again. We have established the parameters of your questioning quite clearly, and you will adhere to those boundaries. I am not interested in feelings or beliefs. This Court concerns itself with the evidence and official analysis at hand, not personal speculation.

...

Understood?

...

Proceed.

[Commander Bastowitz]

I did, though. Your pardon.

[Board Advocate]

Excuse me?

[Commander Bastowitz]

I did believe it was a timely order.

[Board Advocate](simultaneous)

That's not pertinent anym—

[Accused Advocate](simultaneous)

Your Eminence—

[Adjudicator]

(chuckles) Well, you've already entered the question into the record. It is Warned, but you may as well hear the answer now.

[Board Advocate]

I withdraw the question.

[Adjudicator]

Declined.

...

Proceed.

[Commander Bastowitz]

At plus eight seconds it was clear that Fleet was displaying sharply anomalous combat behavior. Plus seventeen seconds it became clear that a detachment from that armada was moving toward the atmospheric boundary with objective unknown. Plus twenty three seconds into the incursion I received an order from Admiral Seersa Kudaibergen via Command Prime to immediately set out with a proximity-assembled strike force from the rear left flank to

      Tiny Planet Filled With Liars

engage what would shortly become the siege installation. As is clearly displayed in the record.

...

I speak quite literally and genuinely when I say I can't conceive how it could possibly have been any more timely than that.

...

The order.

[Adjudicator]

...

Fellow?

[Board Advocate]

...

...

...

What was your professional assessment of the likely tactical outcome matrices as your strike force approached the lens structure?

[Commander Bastowitz]

Death. But hopefully as little as possible.

[Board Advocate]

Explain.

[Commander Bastowitz]

My TEF was a fraction of what would be required to zero out the threat, that much could be assessed immediately. I issued orders to prepare for ramming tactics from the moment we set out. I saw no other plausible decision tree spread ending in a blue matrix scenario within the temporal constraint thresholds. It was not yet apparent that the lens structure would lower its orbit into range of ground emplacements and spike the TEF and KR curves to replant the decision tree.

...

So I expected people to die, but hoped it would be few, and quickly enough to prevent any action against the planet's surface, although it became apparent that was not possible when the lens was completed and went Scry actionable while we were still underway.

...

I must state again that the determinative tactical context did not arise from the Admiralty, it stemmed directly from the consequences of the prior scouti—

[Board Advocate](simultaneous)

Your Eminence, honestly—

[Adjudicator](simultaneous)

That will be quite enough, Commander.

[Accused Advocate](simultaneous)

Louelen, please.

[Adjudicator]

The assertions of archive fiction will *not* tread these Steps. I have apprised you of this before. You are now Warned, Commander.

...

...

...

(sighs)

Next question.

/|\

     TINY PLANET FILLED WITH LIARS

[Board Advocate]

My understanding is that there were multiple avenues of operational disruption in the course of both this incursion and the previous engagement in March. The loss of the bulwark unit alone involved an incident of startling insubordination on … the … part of a Defensive Officer aboard UFD Martial Horizons 3, who misused engineering equipment and executed an act of near-sabotage through unauthorized—

[Admiral Kudaibergen]

Advocate, in *my* understanding that DO saved an enormously expensive mammoth-class boat through creative and heroic action executed with split-second precision under extraordinary combat conditions, and was in no way involved in the PD breakdown which lead to the destruction of that bulwark. They are a genuine hero of inventory attrition prevention. In all other regards, I would love to answer questions relating to the training and operations of individual units in other Divisions, as soon as I am given the authority to determine how those activities are carried out. Lest you forget, I am in *Prime* Command of the fleet in its whole assembly of Divisions, not literal. Perhaps you intend to question the left Flank Admiral, who, you may recall, *does* happen to participate in daily command of 4th Division activities, including training and discipline.

[Adjudicator]

Fellow, I suspect you may not realize that you appear to be flailing. Explain yourself.

[Board Advocate]

(huffs) I hardly think it's appropriate to display bias on the part of the Court. With respect. I humbly beg your forgiveness for faltering while making a case that is in actuality so obvious to perceive. It can only be due to a failing on my own part.

[Adjudicator]

Quite so. Proceed.

[Interviewer]

(snorts)

[Board Advocate]

...

...

...

Why did you feel it was necessary to execute the same flank abort maneuver for the second time in as many consecutive months?

[Admiral Kudaibergen]

It was *not* the same flank abort maneuver, and was not performed for the same reasons, as I have clearly explained to you several times already. In addition, the eastern quadrant was neither the source *of* nor remedy *to* the anomalous activity at the left flank, *especially* with regards to the siege installation.

[Board Advocate]

Admiral, I just find it *so difficult* to believe that after decades of operational stability, *your* tenure happens to coincide with a sudden epidemic of tactical failures. I'm quite—

[Accused Advocate](simultaneous)

You *dare*, while sworn to oath—

[Adjudicator](simultaneous)

Thank you *very* much—

[Admiral Kudaibergen](simultaneous)

I *will* answer the question.

...

The Stability Principle of Fleet Eternal operations is not in dispute here. But that stability does not exist in a state of null context. It is not fixed in *theory*. It is a *dependent* and *operational* variable. Dependent on consistent tactical input from Alpha Vector Defense Corps *in its entirety* in order to maintain. Throughout *both* monthly engagements.

...

When a new stimulus is fed into that paradigm a behavior shift in Fleet is eventually inevitable. When new *behavior* is fed in, the same.

...

Inevitable. I have submitted command expositions on this topic to CBO on multiple occasions. It's quite possible that the ramifications of this will play out for years. *Years*, Advocate. Your very frame of reference is academically obsolete, I do not understand why you'd use it.

[Board Advocate]

I don't see how your pet theories are relevant to the attentions of this Court, and I have other questions to get to.

[Admiral Kudaibergen]

That operational stasis is the *only* reason we survive at all. I—

...

Your Eminence, I insist on presenting the authorized sensor analysis to the Court. In my own defense. Now.

[Accused Advocate](simultaneous)

Admiral, *please* just let me do my work. We may regret this.

[Board Advocate](simultaneous)

Absolutely not! The classifications alone—never mind that it is *not* your pl—

[Adjudicator]

Silence. Advocates and Accused, stand before the dais. Now.

...

Pause transcribing.

...

...

...

[thirty-two seconds of incidental spectator noise]

...

...

...

[Security Officer]

Come with me, please.

[Interviewer](whispering)

What?

[Court Marshal]

This way, please.

[Interviewer](whispering)

What are you talking about? I have—

[Security Officer]

Your presence is no longer authorized. Come with us.

[Interviewer]

What are you *talking* about, this is the goddamn observation terrace, I have every—

[Court Marshal]

You will lower your voice or be sanctioned. Goodbye.

[Interviewer]

Don't touch—

[audible closing doors]

[Interviewer]

What the fuck do you think you're doing? I have a CERT! Give
me your service identification, right the fuck—

[Security Officer]

Your belongings will be inspected before you depart.

[Interviewer]

No, GET your hands off that. Look, I've turned it off. I'll put it—

[muffled rustling]

[Interviewer](muffled)

—in my pocket.

[Security Officer](muffled)

This way.

[Interviewer](muffled)

You're going to have a lot of explaining to do once COAT—

...

...

What?

...

...

...

I don't care *what* you've fucking seen [inaudible] —cking evening report, I haven't been charged with [inaudible] *thing*. Fuck those boot— [inaudible] And! Even if I were, Cert authority—

[muffled rustling]

[Security Officer](muffled)

Right here.

[rustling]

[Security Officer]

Thank you. Right next to the rest.

[Interviewer]

Fine. Fine! You fucking prick.
[recording ends]

EPILOGUE

35

The Interviewer, Various
Pleiades Tower, Penthouse Supreme

WELCOME BACK.

As you know, it is with some great reluctance that I agreed to write this afterword for the second edition reprint, which COAT will shortly issue in honor of the first anniversary of my inaugural Audit. However, it is my sincere hope that doing so now will waylay some of the most frequent (and frequently annoying) questions which I still continue to receive with regards to the events of the previous spring and first summer.

With so much that's happened in the year and a half since, I worried that it might be difficult to explore my own memories of that earlier time with enough impact to make the effort worth attempting. But, perhaps unsurprisingly, I've found that I can put myself right back in those rooms with only the barest effort. I fear, even for a memory like mine, that those four months shall remain singular in their clarity for the rest of my days.

In any case.

Many of you have inquired about Bart, especially in the earliest months; fearful that his cooperation with my investigation would have led to professional consequences. Such fear is, of course, wholly justified. Thankfully I am happy to report that, as in many cases where those who aided my efforts are concerned, the notoriety Bartimus has accumulated appears to have insulated him from any meaningful retaliation, despite the coterie's best efforts. In fact, though the Corps' policy of a Grade III ceiling for all Scries remains intact (and there was never any doubt to that, baseless rumors notwithstanding), Bartimus *has* received a "soft promotion" and is now acknowledged as the titular senior-most Scry in the Alpha Vector Operations Center; salary and privileges unchanged. I do not say lightly that this development was only the least important of the several which occurred in the weeks after you took to the streets in such fury. This timing is not providential.

As to the Third Street AAS, Hector has asked me to reiterate what he has "already told you fuckers a million times." Namely, that your interest is lovingly appreciated, but the Society is no longer accepting membership applications, and can not admit the general public to its facilities, so don't fucking show up there begging to get inside for a picture, and thank you. However, its members remind you that the Rue Boulevard Commemorative Gift Shop remains open 28 hours per day, and you are welcome to visit InDist 12 to take home your own souvenirs at any time. Finally, Vemda particularly notes that there are dozens of other Federation Societies in that quadrant, many of which would be thrilled to take on new members.

Now to Abby and Jieun. Outlandish (and inexplicable) rumors to the contrary, they are not in hiding (from what? I've asked again and again, even while knowing popular conspiracy will never proffer such logic). However, they *certainly* are not interested in your attentions, but do pass along that they are quite touched by them just the same. They have an account open at the Service Member Memorial Fund in Caio's name, with automatic partial distribution to the Crater Zone Survivor's Pool —any attention you insist on giving them ought to be directed there, and there alone. Please respect their privacy, they do not seek your eye. Rest assured, I maneuvered them into accepting ownership of one of my investment penthouses during the previous second summer, after they'd

 Tiny Planet Filled With Liars

agreed to stay there "temporarily" following the lens assault. They remain there, safely idle in comfort. At Abby's insistence we have set up a rent-to-own scheme following her refusal to take my offer of an outright gifting deed. But until now, Abby has not realized that I simply deposit her monthly payments back into an account held in Jieun's name. Now she knows. *Deal with it, Abby.* See you at dinner next weekend, you stubborn old fool. Sorry for blowing our cover, Jieun. Promise I'll make it up to you.

Lieutenant Junior Grade Kekoa, predictably, is doing just fine after the dismissal of all charges. I'm given to understand that multiple contracts have already been negotiated with the live entertainment cartel, awaiting the day when Naomlo finally manages to worm out of the remaining Corps indenture and begin a career as "the shiniest fucker fuckin' remote combat host YOU FUCKERS EVER FUCKIN' SEEEEEN!"

And both Admiral Kudaibergen and Rear Admiral Bastowitz have kindly provided all the cooperation you might rightfully expect to be given to the Office of the Auditor.

/|\

Now to the real reason I know you're all here. The fall of Crowley Vanderbilt.

I do not understand what possible details you believe are missing from the already extensive coverage of same, but I do understand the urge to hear firsthand testimony, and will not deny that to you any longer.

In fact, said events occurred the very same day I'd received news of the overwhelmingly positive consumer survey results that had just been released. You'll be happy to know that, as promised, I did indeed claim the annual consumer sentiment bounty last year. I have long since distributed that award through varying donations to neighborhood organizations around the world.

I cannot express with enough sincerity how grateful I am to your response. May you never understand the full and necessary weight of the political cover it provided to me after those terrible weeks following the first publishing run.

Still, an aftermath did inevitably arise.

Although I know my residence was not the only site of violence that day, it is my firm belief that the release of the consumer sentiment surveys did trigger Vanderbilt's decision to act irrationally. Indeed, until that moment it seemed quite apparent that my report had failed, and that certain forces within the Corps would succeed in their attempts to first discredit, then erase its findings. Though I had already begun to receive some of your reader tips, they were but a smattering initially, and provided no sense of the true audience. But with that first confirmed news that this report had been not just read, but *believed* by millions, any such hopes of my non-achievement on the part of political conspirators would have been dashed.

Mira had promptly warned me that she planned to step up certain security routines in response, but I could not bring myself to take her alerts with even marginal seriousness. What possible breed of true idiocy could lead Vanderbilt to believe that another attack on *me*—still object of roiling media obsession at the time—would go unremarked?

But when Gazala and Taara both sprinted into the penthouse from the outer hallway that afternoon, I nonetheless grasped what was happening immediately.

This was confirmed when Taara said tightly, "They come."

Gazala nodded. "We saw the lift queue. One minute, maybe two."

   TINY PLANET FILLED WITH LIARS

I followed behind them as they rushed with Mira into my office space. "What do you mean? Who's coming? It can't be Crowley, what— what are you doing?"

The trio were rapidly pulling up the flooring near Bart's desk, and started prying at the modular cover that had been installed by the work crew when they'd upgraded the suite's electrical conduits.

Behind us urgent pounding began echoing through the suites from the front door.

I heard Stann move to the annunciator and begin speaking into the view screen.

He said meekly, "Hello?"

"Open up! Constabulary!"

"Hi! No, sorry, we don't need security. We only accept liaison with Dominion regional forces, we're already on file at their office, call them, thanks!"

"DON'T—"

Stann deactivated the view screen and turned to look at me, as I'd moved to stand in the office doorway, trying to watch both areas of concern at once.

He checked his utility belt and remarked to Jin, "Holy shit, what is that, like thirty? Someone's bored."

The pounding redoubled.

Stann put an expression of haughty annoyance on his face and turned back to reactivate the view screen. "NO LOCALS! NO BLITHERING DISTRICT BEATS! GO 'WAY, GO BOTHER SOME PLEBS OR I'LL GET MY BOSS, DAMN IT!"

I watched in utter confusion as Gazala slipped into the conduit workspace (I hadn't even known there *was* space in there) and disappeared below the floor.

Mira and Taara spun around and rushed past me toward the foyer, Mira saying sharply, "Get in the office and shut the door."

I dearly wish I'd listened to her.

Stann left the front doorway, and after a few moments of silence while the team continued arranging itself, the lacquered wood began shaking with impacts again.

Jin walked into the foyer and mutely waited for several seconds before placing his hand next to the annunciator and saying casually, "Hello."

The Constable's voice hitched. "I—uh, we require entry."

"For what?" Jin tapped the view screen impatiently.

Nearby, Mira was a flurry of hand signals to Taara and Stann as they positioned themselves at opposite ends of the foyer, her eyes locked on the view screen over Jin's shoulder.

"Do not question me, boy! OPEN UP!"

"One moment please." Jin looked over his shoulder at Mira and nodded before returning his attention to the door. "Identification please?"

"What? OPEN UP!"

"We haven't ordered food, wrong floor, have a good night."

"OPEN THE FUCK UP!"

"Identification *please*!"

I could see the view screen go black and Jin reached for his sidearm while dashing away from the door, barking, "Brace!"

A moment later my front wall, painstakingly adorned in hand-applied #28 million fractal tapestry, bubbled inward then shattered afore the shockwave of a shaped pressure charge, setting my head into a ringing bell.

A disorganized mob of uniformed bodies spilled through the ragged portal, met by a cacophonous, zippering rip in my ears as sidearms opened up from both ends of the foyer and the drawing room, where Jin and Mira had taken position behind overturned tables. The Constables almost seemed to pass over a trip wire as soon as they set foot on the foyer floor—each immediately tilting forward to crash face-first into the tiles, blood already pooling around their scattered shapes.

I fell to my knees and scrabbled backward, screaming in terror.

A second, smaller wave appeared in the hallway through the smoky ruins of the front wall, and one of them began to raise a military-grade bunker demolisher onto her shoulder when another zipper echoed from outside the suite and the line of Constables toppled sideways, the air suddenly silent in their wake.

A moment later Gazala strolled up behind them, still reloading, and waved at me through the dust cloud. "Hi! All good, folks? Aww, don't cry."

I wept wildly.

/|\

Even then, I sincerely doubt that episode would have led to any involvement with Crowley Vanderbilt at all, in the absence of one key mistake. In fact, I think it would have been astounding if he'd even been *implicated* in an official investigation, were such an alternate reality to be true instead.

No, what saved my life for the final and ultimate time wasn't the fact that several Constables carried illicit military-grade assault weaponry. It wasn't even the fact that nearly half of them carried portable body shackles and bootleg garrotes, or that several of their corpses exhibited tattoos from unauthorized Constabulary coterie clusters. No.

My safety now is simply and solely due to that poor, blessed, stupidly modest (and seemingly hastily assigned) fucker who'd apparently only had time to tug an ill-fitting Constabulary suit over his usual work overalls, which were obediently tagged with the laundry return information for Vanderbilt Ascendant, Incorporated; janitorial department, Palace Equinox; to which it was promptly delivered nine months later following Vanderbilt's treason conviction, in order to recoup the #241.68 missing inventory penalty the corporation's liquidation drawdown warden had levied against Alpha Vector Defense in the meantime.

Glory to the Returns.

/|\

As to Bart's experience in the Alpha Vector Operations Center that same afternoon, it is only by supposition that I can imply Vanderbilt is linked to it, as well. Because of course Alpha Vector Defense has released not a single additional word on the matter, even to me, even in my current appointment; and there is certainly no sign of any additional charges amended to Vanderbilt's prisoner record. The near second-to-second match between the AVOC "disruption" and the arrival of the Constabulary in my penthouse remains, officially, coincidence.

At the time Bartimus was still being bureaucratically punished for his participation in my investigation, and so had been roped into the drudgery of overseeing the calibration of yet another batch of new model desks as they were installed in the AVOC upper balcony. Otherwise he would have had no reason to be in the OC at all that day.

I can not offer—and make no *claim* to offer—any additional evidence that might contradict the official report. The record of an interpersonal conflict escalated into physical brawl in The Pit remains unchallenged, and I include myself among the number of those placated by such explanation.

All I can say is that Bart continues to insist with utter certainty that when the group of Grade XV technicians threw their compatriot up onto the RAAWR dais that day to pin him down and subdue him, Bart saw a destroyer-class incendiary railgun round strapped to the man's chest, and a small device of some kind held in one hand.

/|\

Finally, I would be remiss not to thank those many of you who submitted tips or information of one kind or another to my public address, as requested. You have duly fulfilled your legal obligations and may rest proud. In your honor I have officially updated all outstanding book licenses of the report to become permanent. They will no longer expire. Previously expired licenses have been reactivated, if for some reason you kept the old archive around.

With the information you provided I was able to confirm several key details about the precise activities of Vanderbilt's little cabal during last spring's engagements. In fact, though I haven't been told such, I do believe three of the counts against Vanderbilt stemmed directly from depositionary testimony I was able to provide in part because of your tips.

So, thank you.

From a personal standpoint, there are two tips which met particular interest.

First was the confirmation of UFD Balabalo's combat record during the February incursion. While I admit there was some relief in discovering that Caio's ship had not been part of Vanderbilt's cabal itself, that did nothing to relieve the impotent fire with which I confronted yet another blameless victim of those crimes. But the only thing Caio was guilty of was serving on a missile cruiser which had been left to watch as its entire screening accompaniment suddenly took off and left it naked to a wall of Fleet energy armaments on that fateful winter day. To be able to tell Abby and Jieun the same was ... well.

The second tip sticks in my mind not for its actionability or indeed even its substance, but only for its many and varied implications, each rife with subtly different flavors of potential foreboding.

It arrived anonymously, and was, perhaps, suitably *brief* in its explosiveness. The note concerned Crowley Vanderbilt's grandmother, recorded inventor of the groundbreaking multi-phase antenna technology which abruptly catapulted the family corporation into the upper reaches of Board politics in the previous century.

The note read, simply:

Helena Vanderbilt was not an inventor, she was a reverse-engineer.

 TINY PLANET FILLED WITH LIARS

36

Madame Zhou

Madame Zhou's House, Kitchen, Ruby District

[Madame Zhou]

You know, just cause you Auditor now don't mean I'm gonna stop calling you fancy jacket, fancy jacket.

[Interviewer]

I know.

[Madame Zhou]

'Specially cause you actually fuckin' fancy jacket again finally, thank Jupiter.

[Interviewer]

Mmm. Thank you ... it *is* a gorgeous fabric, isn't it? Look at this thread count, see here? Hardly even a seam. Remarkable.

[M.Z.]

Alright, calm down. If you roll it up and start fucking that sleeve in my kitchen Zhou gonna charge it rent, swear to Jupiter.

[Int.]

(gasps) Do you *know* how expensive it is to have this thing pressed? Good god. I hate even sitting *in* it. What a horrible thought.

[M.Z.]

(laughs)

Good, go get drunk tonight and pay rent to one of my others, then. Works off your debt coming through them just as well as through you, don't it?

...

Anyway, plenty for you to celebrate. You deserve it.

(cackles)

But not as much as I do.

[Int.]

Mm-hmm.

...

I don't pay debt on investments, as you very well remember.

[M.Z.]

(chuckles)

[Int.]

You know Zhou, somehow I don't think you'd need it to begin with.

[M.Z.]

Fuck that supposed to mean?

[Int.]

(chuckles)

...

I ... ah, I hate to insult you by even admitting to it, except now I'm so goddamn curious I have to know.

...

I've looked into your finances and there is absolutely *no* sign of any access to such significant funding. Who the fuck is paying your bills, Zhou?

...

With all my respect to your lovely House, the numbers aren't even *plausible* to project, much less feasible to calculate. Especially not with your ... extracurricular habits.

[M.Z.]

EH! EH! NOBU! YOU FUCKIN' SHITTING BARNACLES THERE OR JUST NORMAL LAZY SELF, EH?

...

SKIM THAT BROTH YOU LUMP.

...

Here, try this.

[Int.]

Who're *you* paying rent to, Zhou? Or what's your side stream? Can't be the House. Can't be.

...

Huh?

[M.Z.]

Fancy jacket, shut the fuck up. Zhou your friend. You need nothing more.

...

Hey, why the fuck you not eating that?

[Int.]

I don't much care for—

[M.Z.]

Zhou gives a fucking shit? *I* made that, not the boys! Eat! Now, or take my sandal to the face. I swear.

[Int.]

(sighs)
Yes, sir.

[M.Z.]

Planet gets a hole blown off it and you think it gives you right to
sass.
(snorts)
Sass your face right into your ass, little shit.

[Int.]

(murmurs unintelligibly)

...

...

...

[two minutes of incidental kitchen background]

...

...

...

[M.Z.]

You going all broody again. Got an egg under there? Good dessert.
(laughs)

[Int.]

Sorry. Just ... ah ... thinking about lies.

[M.Z.]

What, you mean oxygen?
(laughs)
Alright, alright. Tell me fancy jacket, what's lie makes you angriest
today?

[Int.]

...

That Crowley did it alone.

[M.Z.]

...

...

...

Mmm.

...

Yes. Good lie.

[Int.]

...

...

...

Zhou ...

[M.Z.]

(sighs)

For fuck sake, fancy jacket, what? Fuckin' what? You like damn puberty brat today, mope, mope, mope, so many secrets on your mind. What? Tell me, but if it's some big secret you think you gotta confess to mommy, I probably already know. Where you been?

(laughs)

For seriously, fancy jacket.

[Int.]

You're a Highlander, right?

[M.Z.]

...

...

...

(snorts)

Do I look like a Highlander to you?

[Int.]

...

Mm ...

...

...

...

I'll be honest, I don't know if I could even describe it to begin
with.

[M.Z.]

(laughs) Yes, welcome to the world. Nobody know what it is anymore, but everybody sure think they know it when they see it. You
know there's like two real Highlanders left, right? And they own
like twenty gift shops each. (laughs) Who the fuck can even tell
anymore?

...

That not even the Highlands anymore, is it? Since forever. Tall
Conifers Retail District or some shit, right? You think Zhou a
Highlander name?

[Int.]

Well ... no.

[M.Z.]

(chuckles)
Damn right. Everybody know it when they see it, though.
(snorts)

...

...

...

People like underestimating other people, fancy jacket. People relax a little when they think someone sound stupid—'specially
when they've already decided you come from a place that don't

   TINY PLANET FILLED WITH LIARS

make nothing but stupid people. Whether you come from there or not.

…

Being underestimated is a terrible thing, fancy jacket. Nobody should have to go through it. *Especially* when it come from pathetic trash like Crowley Vanderbilt.

…

But if you gonna be underestimated, you better fucking sure use it to your advantage. And why should I get all disadvantage and no advantage just because I born with a "Highlander" face? Hm?

[Int.]

No, I quite agree.

[M.Z.]

(snorts)
Well of course *you* do.

…

Take Petre, there. Perfect example of underestimating.

[Int.]

Really? Petre?

[M.Z.]

Sure. You might look at him and think he nothing but a ball sack hanging from an empty gourd—

…

No, actually, you'd be right then.
(cackles)
FUCK YOU, PETRE!
(raucous laughter)

[Int.]

(chuckles)

Jupiter above. Poor Petre.

...

I mean, that face is *some* consolation certainly, but you're awfully mean to him. Especially as his employer. He's not even indentured, I don't ... really ... actually understand why he's still—

[M.Z.]

(laughs) No, what? Petre is sub. Very, very sub.

...

Very, very sub. He likes. He once tried to pay *me* to abuse him more at work, because he bored, says it gets his pebbles rollin' to occupy the day.

...

(laughs)

For a while I let him think he paying me to be mean to him, stupid idiot never notice I put it right back in his paychit every month under "adjustments." Moron.

[Int.]

Oh my god!

[M.Z.]

(laughs) I said I gave it back!

[Int.]

No it's—I, uh, I'm familiar with an arrangement like that. Though I haven't admitted to it yet.

(sighs)

...

     TINY PLANET FILLED WITH LIARS

Still, awfully generous of you to just give it back to him after he
offered it to you freely, if stupidly. I see charity is a habit for you,
despite appearances.

[M.Z.]

(snorts)

What, I'm gonna steal rent from myself? Idiot. No wonder you so
shit with money until Zhou come along. Don't know shit.

…

Petre and I together very long time. Nobu too. I try to get them
both other work now and then, they never want though. Petre especially, he likes it here. That's why he works so much for me, he
doesn't take any customer who can't be mean enough to him, but
also he gotta be able to trust them, right?

…

(snorts)

Petre could never make a life just on his backside. No way. He's
happy here. From the kitchen he can be picky with customers and
still have some place to rest his stupid fucking head at night.

…

OH!

[Int.]

JUPITER above, what?

…

Goddammit Zhou, don't do that to me, you know the month I've
had.

[M.Z.]

(chuckles) Sorry. Here, take this. To remember, fancy jacket.

[Int.]

Remember what?

[M.Z.]

NO! Jupiter—

[Int.]

Zhou! You're going to put me in the fucking hospital! No more sudden movements at my face, *please!*

[M.Z]

(laughs) I'm sorry, I'm sorry, but you idiot, who the fuck raise you? You don't open gift in front of me like that, Jupiter above. Not one like *this*. Is *commemoration bond* gift. Open it at home. Stupid baby. You wanna give me bad luck for thirty years? How rude? (laughs) Fuck you?

[Int.]

(chuckles)
Oh. Of course, you're right, I'm sorry. Of course not. Never, my dearest Zhou. Thank you most sincerely.

[M.Z.]

You put that on your bedblock.

[Int.]

I, uh, actually have sort of a minimalist aesthetic in—

[M.Z.]

Shut the fuck up.

[Int.]

(laughs) Okay, put the sandal down. I'll put it on the block.

...

I mean, don't you think it'd be more sentimentally relevant to put it on my desk in the new office, if it's from you? Wouldn't that be —(laughs) okay, okay, I understand.

...

      Tiny Planet Filled With Liars

Fuck.

…

I mean this feels like textile, and the office plans *do* have more of a *cottage* theme in th—

[audible clinking glass]

[M.Z.]

Here.

…

Salute.

[Int.]

Mm. Thank you.

…

To you.

[M.Z.]

And you.

…

…

…

Mmm. Tasty.

…

Cheer up, fancy jacket. It's only the end of the world.

[Int.]

(sighs)

Drink to that.

…

…

…

I guess that explains Nobu's standing too, then?

[M.Z.]

What? No. Nobu not sub, he just a fucking idiot.
(laughs)

[Int.]

Oh.

[M.Z.]

Nobu dumb as a goddamn boulder, but he likes doing hard boring
work.

...

...

I mean, maybe Nobu a *little* sub.

[Int.]

What do you mean?

[M.Z.]

He come here and get yelled at, he go home and get yelled at, he in
street and get yelled at 'cause his stupid ass just standing there in
middle of sidewalk or some stupid shit ... he never seem to mind.

...

Stop trying to put him in your fuckin' glossary, fancy jacket. Some
people just have a purpose and they live it. Let the man have a goddamn purpose.

...

Here, watch this, I'll throw a bone. Free of charge.

...

HEY PETRE! EAT SHIT! 'CAUSE YOU LAZY FILTHY SHIT!
FUCK YOU!

(cackles)

   Tiny Planet Filled With Liars

GLORY
to
the
RETURNS
03:42

to
Grandma

to
Andy

to
Citrine & Sidney

<u>AUTHORIZED ABBREVIATIONS & ACRONYMS</u>
<u>GLOSSARY</u>

AAAG [NVIA] — Authorized Abbreviations and Acronyms Glossary, in AAAG context

AAR — After Action Report

AAS [SR, AV "ass"] — Amateur Astronomical Society, in civilian context

AASF [NVIA, AV "the Federation"] — Amateur Astronomical Society Federation, in civilian context

AV — Alternate Verbalization, in AAAG context; see also "NVIA"; see also "SR"; see also "VAS"

AVDC [NVIA] — Alpha Vector Defense Corps

AVOC [verbalized "AY-vok"] — Alpha Vector Operations Center

AXAB [verbalized "axe-AB"] — Axial Abort, in fleet and corresponding unit orders context

CBO — Central Board Oversight

CCIC [SR STRONGLY PREFERRED, informal AV "SEA-sick"] — Command Combat Information Center

CHAVD [NVIA, informal AV VAS] — Court Halls of Alpha Vector Defense

CI — Consent Information, in legal context

COAT [VAS] — Central Office of Applied Thought

DAP [VAS] — Deviant Approach Pattern, in fleet analysis context

DD [SR, AV "Double D" <u>NOT</u> authorized] — Direct Drive, in fleet and corresponding unit orders context

DO [SR, AV "the d-OH"] — Defensive Officer, in personnel context; see also "DO"

DO — Defensive Operations, in departmental and unit context; see also "DO"

EC [SR, derogatory AV "echh" <u>NOT</u> authorized] — Engineering Control, in departmental and unit context

EOY [NVIA] — End Of Year

ETA — Estimated Time of Arrival

FHG — Field Hardening Generator

HQ — Headquarters

IDC — Intellectual Dominion Cert

KR [NVIA preferred, SR authorized] — Kill Rate, in fleet operations and analysis context

LTD. [NVIA] — Limited, limited to corporate usage

NONCON [VAS] — Non-Consensual

NVIA [SR, AV "No Virgins In Alpha" **NOT** authorized] — Never Verbalized In Abbreviation/Acronym or with SR, in AAAG context, one should speak full unabbreviated words <u>ONLY</u>; see also "AV"; see also "SR"; see also "VAS"

OA — Office of the Auditor, in governmental context

OC — Operating Center, in fleet and Corps context

OIT — Officer In Training

PD — Point Defense

PPG — Primary Power Grid, in engineering context

PTS [SR, AV "Piss To Shit" **NOT** authorized] — Physical Training and Supplementation

RAAWR [VAS] — Remote Acquisition Automatic Weaponry Replay

RET. [NVIA] — Retired, in rank context

SAR [verbalized "sah-r"] — Search And Recovery

SOP [VAS, AV SR] — Standard Operating Procedure

SR — Standard Recitation, in AAAG context, verbalize acronym or abbreviation by speaking individual letter names in written order; <u>one should default to SR for all verbalizations unless specifically instructed otherwise, SR is only notated in AAAG when contextually necessary</u>; see contrasting "VAS"; see also "AV"; see also "NVIA"

SSAS [verbalized "SS-ass"] — Sluts Scries And Stars, in AAS context

STS [SR, AV "Skin To Skin" <u>NOT</u> authorized] — Ship To Ship, in fleet context

SUC [VAS, AV SR] — System Unified Code

TDNF — Total Down Net Force, in fleet operations and analysis context

TEF [SR, AV VAS] — Total Effective Firepower, in fleet operations and analysis context

TTK — Time To Kill, in fleet operations and analysis context

UFD — Unified Fiduciary Dominion

UTS — Unified Time Stamp

VAS [verbalized "vass"] — Verbalized As Suspected or as one would naturally pronounce the whole 'word' formed by the acronym or abbreviation, in AAAG context; see contrasting "SR"; see also "AV"; see also "NVIA"

Book Hangover Hair of the Dog Playlist - TPFWL

1. "Star Waves" — *M83*

2. "Wait" — *M83*

3. "Upward To The Moon (Instrumental)" — 白无瑕,
Zi De Guqin Studio

4. "Pack Up Your Troubles In Your Old Kit Bag
(And Smile, Smile, Smile)" — *The Robert Mandell Singers*

smapublishing.com/playlists

Presented in suggestion and purely for personal entertainment purposes. No affiliation is implied or has been sought.

Help the series grow!
Kindly
LEAVE A REVIEW AT YOUR FAVORITE BOOKSTORE
today!

ALSO OUT NOW
Stan, Stan, the Bacteria Man

Coming 2021

Stand on the Rains

—a Fleet Eternal story—

smapublishing.com/newsletter

Blog Tour Guest Post
Unrated Edition!
Filthy and Raw!

<u>or</u>
"Interview with the Author,
by The Interviewer,
as written by the Author"

See even more guest posts at <u>smapublishing.com/media</u>!

[Interviewer]

Alright, alright. Why are we doing this again?

[Stephen M.A.]

Revenue.

[Interviewer]

Ah ... right. I guess you did warn me this was coming, didn't you.

[Stephen M.A.]

Hey, could you—

(sighs)

Could you not break the fourth wall *instantly*? I mean, come on. I'm trying to do a thing here.

[Int.]

Hold on, I've heard that line—this is just repeating that thing you already did right? With the blog tour guest posts?

[SM.A.]

Uh, no, not repeating. *Repurposing*. Anyway, most of it's completely rewritten, and I only used a few snippets from those promo pieces to begin with. This is *inspired by*, because I still need the ability to capture user traffic in order to—I gave exclusive rights to *them* for *those*—see, look up there, I'm gonna do this *here*, and then I've linked to *their* blogs that *I* wrote from *my* site and send people *there* first, and—you know, it's complicated. Metrics. Referrals. Graphs. Draconian user data exploitation paradigms. There's this fucking orange dotted line—okay, you know fucking what, I couldn't fucking curse when I did those guest posts, and I like to fucking curse. Okay? Also there's supposed to be a second book here already, for sampling from so that I can establish a revenue loyalty chain but *clearly* that's nowhere near being finished and—that's the fucking story. Alright? Holy fucking shit.

[Int.]

This is not news to me.

[SM.A.]

Yeah, no shit. Just ask the first fucking question already. Goddammit. I can do this without you just as easily, you know?

[Int.]

Please.

[SM.A.]

Sit down.

[Int.]

Also that bit doesn't work anymore, you've proven quite extensively that you literally cannot do this without me. You never came up with another marketing concept, remember? About five thousand words and half a dozen guest spots worth of proof that the joke doesn't work, so far, as I recall.

[SM.A.]

Oh my god.

...

Hey good soft CTA callback, though.

[Int.]

You wrote it.

[SM.A.]

Enough.

...

First question. God it's taking a lot longer to get started this time, isn't it?

[Int.]

Well you were racing the pre-launch promo deadline then, you're killing time to avoid hitting the publish button now. Have a little discipline and maybe I'll get *to* it already, eh?

...

...

...

[SM.A.]

Shit, I really thought I was gonna let you do it.
(laughs) I didn't, though, did I.

[Int.]

You sure did not.

...

...

...

Holy shit. Okay, *first question.* I am *asking the first question now, you will answer it, and then we will publish.* Yes?

[SM.A.]

...

...

...

(laughs)

Oh my fucking god who am I, Little Britain? Once was enough! There's probably only one person out there who's even realized I'm still making the same bad joke here! They'd need to have already read the other guest spots to fully get it, then they'll realize it wasn't particularly good to begin with! What a waste of valuable product real estate! And their time! Isn't the whole point of this so that I can build loyalty among superfans and shame them into <u>signing up for my newsletter</u> (smapublishing.com/newsletter)? How the fuck is this—
(laughs)
This bullshit has gone on so long they've probably had to flip a page by now!
(snorts) Oh my god what am I doing.

[Int.]

I really, sincerely, quite deeply concur. Let's *do* get on with it.

...

...

...

Don't you fucking dare. I can fucking *see you thinking* about the rule of threes.

[SM.A.]

Well the thing is I'm not a comedian, so I never really think about it while writing. But it's just such an inherently organic narrative

 Tiny Planet Filled With Liars

mechanism that it tends to happen a—Hey! Look at fucking that, you basically asked me a question. We're past it.

[Int.]

Well thank Jupiter for that, then.

...

That was more than three times though, by the way.

[SM.A.]

WHAT? Let me see the fucking readout.

...

(muttering)

One, two—

...

Oh my fucking—okay, we're starting over. Four times isn't funny.

[Int.]

Second question—you realize this whole guest posts gag is now just documentation of a descent into quarantine madness, right? At least those other ones are hosted by the blogs! *We're* paying for the per-page bandwidth and printing costs, here.

...

I mean, you're paying.

...

I'm still pretty sure there's a way for you to give me royalties even though I'm a product of your imagination, though. Don't fucking think I've let *that* go just because you're trying to waste our entire goddamn week on twee publicity and I'm trapped in here with you, suffering in the meanwhile.

[SM.A.]

...

Oh, good stinger tag for the marketing copy.

...

"Descent ... into ... quarantine madness."

...

Mm, no. Actually, that doesn't work for marketing copy for the book. I'll have to use it somewhere else. Oh! I know. I'll put it at the start of the line you just got done saying.

...

...

Oh, good stinger tag for the marketing copy.

[Int.]

(sighs) Holy shit.

...

And will you *stop* fucking giggling? Okay, that snort isn't even in the transcript. This isn't *funny*, it's a fucking hostage scenario, godammit!

...

...

...

(sighs) Sonofabitch.
Alright, is that what this all is?

...

Huh?

...

You're tired of quarantine?

...

Yeah?

[SM.A.]

(grunts)

     TINY PLANET FILLED WITH LIARS

[Int.]

Hey, big guy, I know. Hey, hey. It's alright. I know. It's been a veeery long time. Even for a hermit like you. You're completely right.

[SM.A.]

(sniffs)

[Int.]

You shouldn't have to be here at *all* anymore, should you?

[SM.A.]

(grunts)

[Int.]

That's right. That's right. Neither of us should. You think I still want to be climbing the walls here inside your fat fucking head? Huh?

...

Of course not.

...

But the world is filled with homicidal typhoid tantrum toddlers it is a literal goddamn zombie movie at the Sunoco and *here we are so let's make the* FUCKING MOST OF IT AND **FINISH THIS FUCKING INTERVIEW ALRIGHT?**

[SM.A.]

Aw, come on.

[Int.]

SIXTEEN MOTHERFUCKING HOURS OF IT! AND DON'T YOU DARE THINK I DON'T NOTICE YOU TRYING TO "EDIT" IT FOR ANOTHER SIXTEEN MORE NOW, BITCH! LOOK! YOU TORTURE ME SO FUCKING MUCH I'M US-

ING CURSES THAT AREN'T EVEN MOTHERFUCKING IN-UNIVERSE! I AM LITERALLY MOTHERFUCKING OUT OF CHARACTER NOW, YOU HAPPY? YOU THINK I CAN'T UNIONIZE JUST BECAUSE I'M FUCKING FIC-TIONAL? LET'S FUCKING TEST THIS SHIT! LET'S GO! YOU THINK I FORGOT THE KNIFE IN MY BACK LIKE TEN MINUTES AGO THAT *YOU* WROTE THERE? GIVE ME THE FUCKING FINGERS ASSHOLE, I'M EMAILING THE FUCKING SFWA AND WGA I FUCKING TOLD YOU I'D FUCKING DO IT. MOVE OVER.

[SM.A.]

Get—GET OFF! How are you even—OW! FUCKING—

[recording pause]

/|\

[SM.A.]

O—okay. Okay. We're ... uh ...

[Int.]

Don't talk about it.

[SM.A.]

Okay. Yeah, okay. You're right.

[Int.]

How much would you say this story was written in reaction to the general arc that ended up describing 2020?

[SM.A.]

Well fortunately "epic shitstorm" has been a very applicable term for quite some time, so it had no functional impact at all. By the

   Tiny Planet Filled With Liars

time the Before Times became the Before Times the story was already more than half finished. The bones of it, anyway.

…

I began writing the book in December of 2019, after a failed experiment in another genre. Sci-fi is where my heart's always been, anyway. And—I mean, *you* know, you were already there at the time, even if I didn't realize it yet. Remember the feast we had that night at Andy's? When I knew for sure the last series had fuckin' CRAAASHED and burned. Rightfully. I was in costume then, why'd I expect anyone to care? I didn't actually. Maybe that was the point. The pointless point. Fuck. Anyway, then psychological breakdown, tears on the FDR out of town, blah, blah, sudden inspiration, wrote the first five chapters by the next morning, whatever. It's been a journey. You don't need to be told.

[Int.]

(snorts)

Yes. I have, as they say, "seen some shit."

[SM.A.]

Sure, but we're through it now.

[Int.]

TBD.

[SM.A.]

Okay, moving on.

[Int.]

So what *did* inspire you to write this story, then?

[SM.A.]

Well, I mean, still—

(gestures broadly at everything)

[Int.]

Ah, I see you are keyed into played out social trends.

[SM.A.]

Yes, since the nation took a fascist turn I do follow the Twatter feeds, but only vaguely, like an old. Anyway, there's no revenue to be found there in my personal experience. As far as I'm concerned it is a unitasking tool built solely for purposes of rage retweeting into the void, which I have done extensively of late. I'll probably deactivate the account entirely soon. I would have already but one time Jemaine Clement liked and retweeted something I said in reply to Sarah Cooper so now the account's in the National Register of Historic Places even though I have like 3 followers and it's this whole thing. I'll keep at it and get that fucker taken down sooner or later, though. I'm quite sure my time there was but a momentary interlude. It has to be, I can't be trusted with it.

[Int.]

Wise. Unlike an old.

[SM.A.]

Mm-hmm.

...

DON'T TRY AND FIND ME THERE I WILL NOT BE. FIND MY AUTHOR PAGE ON FACEBOOK. I KNOW IT IS THE LITERAL HELLMOUTH OF DEMOCRACY BUT IT'S THE ONLY PLACE I CAN PROPERLY STAY IN TOUCH WITH YOU RIGHT NOW UNLESS YOU <u>JOIN MY NEWSLETTER</u> (SMAPUBLISHING.COM/NEWSLETTER) INSTEAD. FUCK.

...

...

   TINY PLANET FILLED WITH LIARS

The basic story here has been the same my entire life, and in my opinion what's happening now is only the inevitable outcome of a path we've been on for a long time. So, really, from my perspective it was just about picking the fictional setting for it all.

[Int.]

Is there any character you particularly identify with? Am I—okay, now that joke *really* doesn't work anymore after the shit you just got done pulling. No, not this time around, buddy. Look, see that shit? I'm still a little OOC from it. No.

[SM.A.]

(sighs)

Yeah.

...

Should we just call it? I guess I'm ready.

[Int.]

(gasps) Oh thank fucking Jupiter. Yes, please and thank you.

[SM.A.]

I'm really going to shit myself if this doesn't sell, though.

[Int.]

I know big guy. I know.

[SM.A.]

I mean, really.

[Int.]

Yeah, I get it, I don't do laundry, the fuck do I care? Let's do this! Posthaste!

[SM.A.]

(sighs)

Go on, then.

[Int.]

And that'll just about do it for us, folks! Thanks so much to [IN-SERT BLOG NAME HERE] for hosting us! Okay, that just doesn't work anymore either. Oh shit, and neither does this next —Grab Tiny Planet Filled With Liars (smapublishing.com/buy) today on Kindle Unlimited! Where you may very well already be reading it, because this is the actual book, not a promotional guest post on a blog!

[SM.A.]

Wow.

[Int.]

Goodbye!

[SM.A.]

Yeah goodbye. What's the point. Probably just deleting the whole fucking book tonight anyw—

[recording ends]

Alright, you've read this far, inexplicably, and beyond all reasonable expectations of user forbearance—you're a superfan, admit it!

Go on. <u>Sign up for my newsletter!</u>
smapublishing.com/newsletter

I promise I won't abuse the privilege. Trust me, it's a near-certainty that I hate *all* forms of communication more than you do. You'll be lucky to hear from me more than two or three times a year! So I've been told; in writing!

I just want to keep you updated on important news about Fleet Eternal, and especially the release of the sequel: **Stand on the Rains, coming 2021!**

Go oooooooooooon.
smapublishing.com/newsletter
Go ooonnnnnnnn!

Please this peak empire economic hellhole gives me no other avenue with even half as much ROI that leads into the monopsonistic wasteland of modern American independent publishing if you leave now I'll lose you forever and die penniless and alone and while I wouldn't necessarily hate the alone part depending on my mood I'm *so* very tired of the pennilessness; you get it.

Come now, did you really read *this* far just to not <u>SIGN UP FOR MY NEWSLETTER</u>?

Go ooooooooon!!
smapublishing.com/newsletter
YEEEEEEEEEEEAHHH!!!!!

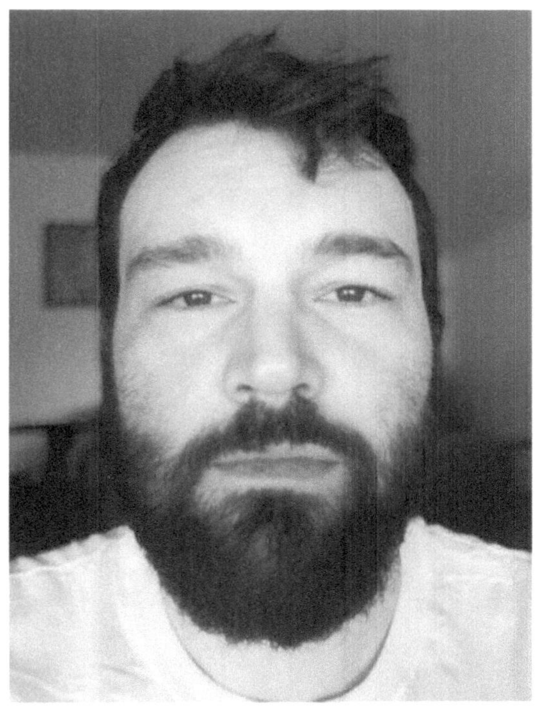

Stephen M.A. is an ex–film student, Great Recession and millennial economy survivor, domestic COVID refugee, and first-generation tribal descendant originating from a reservation in big sky country. He now lives and writes in the Northeastern United States after a long and broken spell in Brooklyn.